The Ship Between the Worlds

JULIA GOLDING

OXFORD

UNIVERSITY PRESS

OXFORD
UNIVERSITY PRESS

Great Clarendon Street, Oxford OX2 6DP

Oxford University Press is a department of the University of Oxford.
It furthers the University's objective of excellence in research, scholarship,
and education by publishing worldwide in

Oxford New York

Auckland CapeTown Dar es Salaam Hong Kong Karachi
Kuala Lumpur Madrid Melbourne Mexico City Nairobi
New Delhi Shanghai Taipei Toronto

With offices in

Argentina Austria Brazil Chile Czech Republic France Greece
Guatemala Hungary Italy Japan Poland Portugal Singapore
South Korea Switzerland Thailand Turkey Ukraine Vietnam

Oxford is a registered trade mark of Oxford University Press
in the UK and in certain other countries

British Library Cataloguing in Publication Data
Data available

ISBN 978-0-19-275483-7

3 5 7 9 10 8 6 4

Typeset in Garamond MT by TnQ Books and Journals Pvt. Ltd.,
Chennai, India

Printed in Great Britain by Cox and Wyman Ltd

CR
F
GOL

For Edward

The Ship Between the Worlds

Contents

CHAPTER ONE
Ship in a Bottle

D avid Jones was in trouble—deep trouble. It was the kind of trouble that would leave him with his face rearranged and his new uniform ruined.

He pounded down Park Road, shirt flying, bag bumping on his shoulder. Seven boys raced after him, pushing the other children out of their way. The gang was led from the front by Jason Rickson, better known as Ricko. An ugly boy with close-cropped hair and small, piggy eyes, not even Ricko's mother could think him good-looking. David had made the mistake of venturing this opinion when the gang had decided to amuse themselves by chucking his sports kit around the playground, leading to the present need to run for his life.

Still, I was honest, even if I do end up getting my head kicked in, David thought grimly as he sprinted ahead of the pack. *Mad but truthful.*

David rounded a corner and scrambled over a wall into the Waterside Estate, landing in a prickly bush in a neighbour's back garden. He bit back a curse. He'd forgotten that rose was there. Now, unless the gang decided to follow him, he was protected by the automatic gates and fence that ringed Waterside. With any luck, they wouldn't have seen exactly where he went over.

'Where's he gone?' snarled Ricko, his voice coming from close by.

'Dunno. Over the wall somewhere,' said one of his gormless lieutenants, getting no thanks for stating the obvious.

Bent double, David's breath was coming in painful gasps. He smothered his mouth with a muddy hand, fearing the gang would detect him. But they were too busy shouting a selection of their favourite insults to hear.

'Geek!'

'Wimp!'

'Moron!'

Humiliated, David shivered in the shelter of the wall, waiting for them to give up. They'd get bored sooner or later if they couldn't see him.

I mean, how long can even ape-brained thugs like them keep shouting at bricks? he wondered.

The answer? Longer than he could have thought possible. Kneeling in the dirt he had plenty of time to reflect on how much he hated them—and himself for running away.

I am so pathetic: an A-starred loser. If running from bullies was a GCSE, I could take it this week and get the top mark.

But what could he do against so many? He had asked himself this so many times over the last few days. He didn't dare to tell anyone at school; Ricko had already warned him what would happen if they caught him bleating to a teacher. As for his mum, she had so many problems at the moment, he didn't want to burden her. It was so unfair! He hadn't done anything to the gang but that didn't seem to matter. Ricko had just chosen him for 'the treatment' because he had turned up in class new and friendless. There was only one boy, Mike Tailor, still mental enough to risk sitting next to him. Mike escaped the bullies because everyone thought him pretty cool for his skill on the football pitch. Sadly, his coolness did not extend to protecting David. David knew he was considered the pits of uncool, the class idiot, the victim.

And after weeks of harassment, he was beginning to believe it too.

'Don't worry, Jonesey: we'll get you tomorrow,' jeered Ricko, knowing full well his quarry couldn't be far away. 'Missin' you already!'

With a parting chorus of insults and laughs, the gang finally left to collect a few ASBOs, mug pensioners, or whatever it was they did when they weren't torturing new boys. Shakily, David got up from his knees to walk home.

There was absolutely nothing good about his new life in Waterside, fumed David, inspecting his scratches. Life here sucked.

Well, that wasn't totally true. He hadn't dared tell anyone for he knew it would sound weird (and right now he didn't want to add 'weird' to his list of shortcomings, there was plenty to be going on with already) but he'd begun to have the most amazing dreams. They were always about the same thing: he was aboard a ship—a ship with billowing sails. He spent each night swaying across its deck, clambering in the rigging and looking out for hours across a starlit ocean. And when he woke, he always thought the salt tang of the sea air lingered in his bedroom for a few moments. They were beautiful, wonderful dreams.

Undeniably weird though.

He let himself in at the back gate and stood looking at his house, still not quite believing it was his home now. Immediately below his bedroom window was the conservatory, tacked on to the back of the house like a white and glass cruise liner berthing at a brick terminal. If he looked to the right, he would see another just like it next door. If he looked the other way, there was another, and another—each house with its own little glasshouse attached to the rear. David knew that his father would not have approved: he would have called the house 'boring'. When Simon Jones had been at home, he had promised his son that, if they moved anywhere, it would be somewhere really special—a lighthouse or a ramshackle cottage by the sea, not a new house in a city as far from the coast as you can get.

But he wasn't here any more, and David and his mum had washed up on the Waterside Estate to face a life without him. Yeah, it *was* true: life here sucked.

The following morning found David hard at work, escaping his worries in the job before him. Running his fingers through his wiry brown hair, he looked happily down on the model floating in a sea of cotton threads and scraps of cloth that littered the surface of his desk. It was not something he told most people but he was really in to making things and was pretty good at it, even if he did say so himself. His current project was almost ready now. When he had fitted the last sail, the miniature ship he had copied from his dreams would be finished. His grandad, a fellow model enthusiast, was coming that afternoon and had promised to help him manoeuvre it into the big bottle David had found to house it. The tricky part was ensuring that the three masts would rise smoothly when he pulled on the thread attached to them. If it worked to plan, the miracle of the ship in the bottle would be complete. He looked forward to his mother's bemused questions as to how he had managed to get such a large thing inside so small a bottle—she would never guess the secret.

'School!' his mother called from downstairs. 'Get a move on, David!'

Reluctantly, he put down the triangular patch of white cotton he had intended for a sail at the prow of his ship. He wished he could stay all day with his model in its glass cocoon but he knew from experience that his mother would make him face school—and Ricko—whatever excuse he invented. He'd previously tried claiming to be ill with most infectious diseases known to mankind, ranging from flu to (on one particularly desperate occasion) plague, but somehow, after clucking sympathetically, his mother always prescribed breakfast and a bracing walk to school as the cure. Heaven help him if he ever was really sick.

Oh well, perhaps today the gang would leave him alone, he thought optimistically.

Who are you fooling? his more cynical side chipped in as he closed his bedroom door.

Later that afternoon, David had reason to feel smug. He had won a small, but, he felt, significant victory for the victims of this world. He had managed to outwit his tormentors by climbing over the playground fence and taking a detour down the canal. For once he was going to have a peaceful and uneventful evening—or so he thought.

'I don't know why you did it.' He recognized his grandad's voice speaking heatedly. David hovered outside the back door, schoolbag over one shoulder, listening. Great, this was just what he needed. An argument. His mother and his grandad—his father's father—did not get on well. He knew better than to walk in on one of their 'family discussions'.

'Of course you know why!' his mother replied, her tone waspish.

'But buying a place like this on land prone to flooding! It's the same everywhere—these new developments—built where they shouldn't be. And the gates—great ugly gates shutting out the riff-raff like me. I have to buzz to come and see my own grandson. You've put him in a prison— a luxurious one but a prison nonetheless.'

'When you've quite finished insulting my home—' said David's mother.

'What was wrong with the old place?' his grandad ploughed on. 'It had so much character—'

'I'll tell you what was wrong with the old place,' she said, finally losing it. 'When your son decided to up and leave his wife and child without so much as a goodbye, I couldn't bear to live there a second longer. What do you think I am? Made of money?'

'We would've helped—'

'No! I don't want your help. I can manage.'

'But can't you see that the boy's not happy here?'

'He'll settle down. It's early days yet. His father's only been gone a few months.'

His grandfather sighed. David was relieved: it sounded as if he was backing down.

'I know, I know, Jean. I'm sorry—I spoke out of turn. You're managing very well, all things considered. I'm worried about Simon too—but he'll be back when he realizes what a fool he's been.'

'Maybe, but I'm not sure I'll want him when he does pitch up.'

'But David will—a boy needs his father.'

David's mum didn't reply to that but thumped something hard on the ironing board.

The storm was blowing over. It was safe to go in. David entered the kitchen and found his grandad sitting with a mug of tea, his mother ironing; both pretending they hadn't just been yelling at each other. He played along, pretending he hadn't heard.

'David, how's my old seadog?' called his grandad, getting to his feet to enfold him in a hug. He had a wrinkled face, brown like a walnut. His bright blue eyes sparkled beneath a crop of white hair, just balding at the crown. His clothes smelt of pipe smoke. David buried his head in his jacket, feeling comforted by the familiar scent. At least Grandad was still here.

Grandad Jones pushed him gently to arm's-length. 'Ready for Operation Restore?'

David nodded. 'Almost.' He was thankful his grandad had not asked him about school.

'Operation Restore?' asked his mother, managing a smile for David. She used to be pretty, but since David's father had left, her face had settled into an almost permanent frown, two deep lines pinching the skin above her nose. Her black hair was beginning to grey at the temples. 'What on earth is that?'

'Ah-ha!' said Grandad mysteriously. 'It's a surprise. Will it be ready by eight bells?'

David checked his watch. That gave him half an hour as it was three-thirty now.

'Yep, should be.'

'Then I'll just finish my tea in the galley and come up and join you.'

'You and your naval language!' said Mum, not entirely pleased. 'Just like Simon.'

Having Grandad in the house was *almost* as good as having Dad back, thought David as he mounted the stairs. Before his father had disappeared, the two of them had enjoyed larking around, taking zany pleasure in their special sea-language like a couple of daft extras who'd wandered off the set of *Pirates of the Caribbean*. They had often fantasized about what it would have been like to be on board the sailing ships of the past. They'd said 'Aaargh!' a lot in stupid accents. Had fun.

The thought of Simon Jones's absence was like a sharp knife sticking in David's ribs. He had not felt whole for many months and knew he had taken to slouching almost as if protecting the wound. Perhaps it was this vulnerability that had attracted Ricko to him like a shark scenting blood in the water. But if so, he didn't know what to do about it as the pain refused to go away.

David was jolted from this bleak train of thought when he opened the door to his bedroom. There it was again: that salty tang from his dreams, but this time in daylight. Where had it come from? He went to the window, but it was closed. All he could see outside were the backs of other houses. Strange.

Turning to the desk, he looked for the triangular piece of material he had been using that morning to make a sail. It wasn't there. He looked under the table. Not there either. Under the books? Under the bed? No. It had vanished. While his bedroom might look to an outsider as if the army had conducted a controlled explosion in his clothes drawers, to him there was a pattern to his own clutter. The sail had definitely been moved.

David's thoughts immediately leapt to blame his mother. She must have come in here to clean despite promising to leave his room untouched until he had finished his secret project. Full of the righteous anger of a son whose privacy had been invaded, he went out onto the landing.

'Mum!' he yelled downstairs. 'Did you go in my room?'

She stuck her head out of the kitchen.

'Don't be silly—I've been at work all day. Anyway, I wouldn't take the risk, who knows what you've got buried under your smelly clothes—the *Mary Celeste*, Shergar, they could all be in there and no one would know.'

'Oh.' David's tantrum was put on hold.

'What's up?'

'Lost something, that's all,' he muttered sheepishly.

'Well, if you kept your bedroom tidy like I told you—'

'Yeah, yeah.' David retreated back into his den.

There was nothing for it: he would have to make another sail. He rifled through the scraps of cloth on the desk, looking for some white material. How weird: the desk seemed to be covered in a fine grit. He bent closer, scraping a sample up on a moistened finger. It was sand—silver sand. How had that got there?

'David, have you finished yet?' called his grandad.

'Nearly!' David shouted back, grabbing the scissors and cutting out another sail. He tried to thread a needle but missed several times. How did his father do it? Remembering, he licked the

12

end of the thread and this time it passed smoothly through. He tacked the sail onto the ship by its three corners. There, that should be it.

His grandad's heavy footsteps could be heard climbing the stairs.

The old man whistled softly behind him. 'Why, David, that's a beauty. It's just like the *Whydah*.'

'The *Whydah*?' David asked, turning his model carefully around in his hands, scrutinizing it from every angle. Its three masts stood straight, each billowing with three sails. The tiny revolving capstan, used to weigh anchor, looked ready for its crew. He had placed little swivel guns along the sides made from matchsticks; each turned on its pivot like the real thing would have done. The cannon on the main deck trundled in and out of the portholes he had cut in the ship's sides. He didn't care if others would think him a bit of a geek making this sort of thing. It was perfect.

'The *Whydah* was a pirate vessel; I thought you must've known that if you copied it so faithfully.'

David shook his head, wondering if he should mention his dreams. But his grandfather was so practical minded, he would probably tease David for admitting to such fanciful ideas. Best to keep them secret.

'I must've seen a picture, I s'pose,' he said with a shrug.

'Well, the *Whydah* sank hundreds of years ago. Why don't you give it a pirate flag?'

'This ship doesn't have a pirate flag,' said David firmly.

'Suit yourself. So, shall we put it in its bottle?'

David nodded and lowered the masts with the cotton rigging he had prepared for this task.

'It's going to be a bit of a squeeze,' he admitted, lifting the glass bottle onto the desk.

'Oh, the ship won't mind. It's always a squeeze on board a sailing vessel, remember?'

'Just space to sling your hammock, no more, no less,' David said with a nod.

'That's how your Jones ancestors used to live when they were at sea. They were packed together like sardines. Unless one of them made it to be captain, of course. Then you got your own cabin.' Grandad pointed to the gaily-painted windows of the stern where David had put his best cabin. 'That's where I'd be. But you, my lad, it's below decks for you!' He pointed at the middle of the ship. 'And if you were disobedient, I'd throw you in the brig.'

David laughed. 'Butt out, Grandad, it's *my* ship: I could throw *you* in the brig for saying that.'

Grandad chuckled. 'Too right, my lad. Don't let any old-timer like me steal your command from under you. Now, shall we let this little lady set sail?'

14

With heads bent together, David and his grandad pushed the ship into the neck of the bottle. Once it cleared the narrow opening, there would be no fishing inside to pull it back out. The boat, masts still lying flat, slid smoothly into the glass sea.

'Now for the moment of truth!' said the old man, settling his spectacles more firmly on his nose. 'Heave away there, my lad!'

Cautiously, David tugged on the cotton. If the thread snapped, the only way to get the ship out for repair would be to smash the bottle. Trembling slightly, the masts rose together, straightening out their crumpled white sails.

'There she goes!' cried his grandad. 'What are you going to name her?' He held a thimbleful of water ready to throw against the bottle.

David pointed. 'I've put the name on already. She's the *Golden Needle*.'

'The *Golden Needle* then,' said the old man, pouring the water on the glass. 'God bless her and all who sail in her!'

CHAPTER TWO
Press-Ganged

David lay on his bed watching the shadows cast by the moonlight rippling on his curtains. His ship-in-a-bottle sat in pride of place on the desk. He was glad it was safe from Ricko's gang here: he'd hate anything to happen to it after he'd spent so much time working on it. Perhaps he'd show Mike, if he ever came round to his home.

The window was open, letting in the spring night air. The drapes billowed gently. They reminded him of the ocean lapping at his feet last summer on what he thought of as 'the last holiday', the one that had brought his world to an end.

He had stood at the water's edge with his father beside him, watching the sailing dinghies gliding across the blue expanse. A tall, strong man dressed in faded denim trousers and shirt, Simon Jones looked at home by the sea. David loved to feel his father's calloused palm resting lightly on his shoulder, sand under his bare feet, and the smell of the sea in the air. He had felt completely happy.

His mother had been sitting in a deckchair, nose buried in a book, content to let her 'two boat-mad boys', as she called them, have their fun. Before coming, Simon had promised to take his son sailing, so David had been talking non-stop to his father, pointing out his favourite yachts, dropping heavy and unrealistic hints as to which he'd like for his eighteenth birthday when the time came, not noticing that he was getting no response. Simon Jones had been distracted since they had arrived on the beach, his eyes losing their focus as if he was looking at something in the distance. David had been too excited by the boats to worry that the attention of his audience was drifting; he only stopped talking when his dad removed his arm from his shoulders.

'Can you see it, David?' Simon asked suddenly.

'See what, Dad?'

Simon shook himself, as if throwing off a dream. His face took on a determined expression.

'I can't put this off any longer. I've got to go now: we're running out of time. Give these to your mum, won't you?' He dropped the car and house keys into David's open palm. 'I won't be long. I've just got to go away for a few days.' He looked guiltily over at his wife and did not quite meet David's eyes.

'Go away?' asked David, startled. 'But you can't: we've only just arrived!'

'I know. I'm sorry. But last night I found out that there was something I had to do. You understand?'

David didn't. He knew his dad could be unpredictable but this was scary.

'You tell your mum I'll be back. I'll contact you in a few weeks to let you know when exactly.'

'A few weeks?' The period was stretching ever longer.

'I'm not sure how long it will take, you see.'

'That's so lame, Dad. Why not tell Mum yourself? Why leave me to tell her?' asked David angrily. 'Tell her now.' He turned round to gesture towards his mother. She looked up and smiled.

'What are you waving at me for, David?' she asked, putting her book down. 'Do you want an ice cream or something? Or perhaps your father's gone to get one already?'

David spun round quickly. His father had disappeared; only the deep imprints in the sand beside him marked where Simon had stood. A rowing boat that had been bobbing on the water a second before had also vanished. Its owner, weighed down with fishing rods, trousers rolled up to his knees, was scratching his head.

'I swear it was here. Did you see what happened to my boat?' the man asked a kid building a sandcastle. The kid shrugged and carried on with his excavations.

David stood still for a moment. He then walked slowly over to his mother and dropped the keys into her lap.

'What does this mean?' his mother asked in confusion, looking up at him as if he could help.

David said nothing, feeling tears welling up inside. He mustn't cry. He was too old to cry and definitely not in front of everyone.

Staring into his face for a moment, his mother threw her book on the ground and ran off down the beach.

'Simon!' she called out, pushing her way through the crowds on the steps by the beach. 'Simon! Where are you?'

David sat at the feet of her deckchair and hung his head, wishing the sea would sweep in and swallow him up.

The pain of that day hadn't left him. It lurked inside him like a tiger slinking through the jungle, springing out at unexpected moments. He and his mother had waited for the promised message, but none had arrived. He punched the pillow. He hated his father for marooning him on the beach. The anger clawed at him, keeping him awake long into the night. All he wanted to do was escape to his dreams of sailing quiet seas, but tonight sleep eluded him.

'I tell you, it's here somewhere,' whispered a voice outside in the garden.

David froze, fist still buried in the pillow. That wasn't his mother—or anyone he knew—it was a man's voice, deep and guttural as if the stranger was more used to growling than talking. It must be a burglar. He threw back his covers and rushed to the window. Cautiously he lifted the edge of the curtain.

'Sssh!' hissed a second voice. 'They'll hear us-ss!'

There were two of them: two shadowy forms down on the path. But more than that. David rubbed his eyes.

No way. Was he dreaming after all?

There, moored to the conservatory, was the *Golden Needle*, shimmering like a vision of an oasis in a desert. The prow was in the garden of number twenty-one, the stern bumping up against the fence of number thirty-three. The sails were furled but David could see quite clearly that there were three masts soaring above him. A flickering light danced on the lawn as if reflected from a half-seen ocean lapping at the hull.

This was impossible.

Impossible or not, he now saw that the men were coming inside—inside *his* house. He panicked. What should he do?

He dived back into bed and hid his head under the duvet, praying that they would not come into his room.

Aren't I the hero? Surely, I can think of something better than this?

But before he could decide what 'better' was, there was a scrape at the door, like the sound of a dog asking to come in. The handle turned and the door creaked open.

'Shushula was right: there it is. A beauty, ain't it?' growled the first man.

'A real gem for the captain's collection,' agreed the second.

'She said she couldn't manage it on her first foraging trip; but she told the truth when she said it's well worth returning for.'

'Aye, that it is.'

David hardly dared breathe as he listened to the two burglars make their way stealthily across his room. There was something strange about their steps: one seemed to be dragging himself along—perhaps he was injured?—the other was bounding softly forward with a steady thump, thump, thump. But what was it they were after? There was nothing of any value in his room. Ricko had had his MP3 player off him weeks ago and even he had turned his nose up at David's new trainers.

There came a rustling from over by his desk and the sound of something being dropped into a sack.

'What about that sheet on the bed, Art?' hissed the second voice. 'The jib still needs patching. That little scrap Shushula salvaged is fit only to mend a moth hole, but the last battle blew a great rent in the sail.'

'Hmm,' the one called Art grunted. 'It will do. Take it.'

To his horror, David felt his duvet being dragged from the bed, revealing him to the two astonished visitors. This was too much for David: not only had they broken into his bedroom, but they had now the brazen cheek to steal his bedclothes!

'Hey, that's mine!' he cried, sitting up and tugging back the duvet. He then saw properly the faces of the two people staring back at him. He gave a muffled scream and let go.

'Dammit, you're not supposed to be able to see us!' cursed the first man—but it wasn't a man. David found himself eye to eye with a crouching monkeyish fellow with purple eyes and long limbs ending in six-fingered splayed hands and feet. He wore only a pair of old breeches, the rest of him being covered with thick brown fur.

'But if he can see us-ss,' said the other, 'then he'll have to come with us-ss. That's the rule.' The second creature was coiled around David's duvet, a great green serpent with a red flickering tongue and a cockerel's comb of golden spikes. David retreated to the end of the bed and gave a terrified moan. He clung onto the bedpost as two hands grabbed his ankles.

'Come on, my landlubber, you're going for a little walk,' growled the monkey-fellow. David kicked hard against the rough hands tight around his feet.

'Mum! Mum!' he shrieked, but his voice was choked and the cry came out as a whisper.

'Halist, help me! This little sprat doesn't want to come into the net,' said Art.

The duvet was bundled over David's head and strong arms gripped his waist. Half-suffocating in his own bedclothes, he was carried from the room. Art loped across the landing, down the stairs, and out into the garden. He dumped David into a basket. Struggling to get free, David found that a coil of something heavy had slithered on top of him.

'Eass-y, lad,' hissed Halist. 'We don't want to be tipped out, do we now?'

The basket began to creak as it was hauled up the side of the vessel David had seen from his window. He lay motionless, still hoping for a chance to escape. The basket swung free for a second before being winched down onto the deck. It tipped over, spilling Halist, the duvet, and David onto the planks.

'Well, well, what have we here?' called out a new voice. It had a ringing tone, well-suited to calling out commands over the howl of a storm. 'Fish, fowl, or friend?'

David looked up into the night sky and saw a man with long russet-red hair, a black plumed hat, and a gold earring. He bent closer to David, holding out a muscular arm with the tattoo of a shark swimming down from his elbow. David was too scared and astonished to move. The man looked like some kind of buccaneering Hell's Angel, and about as friendly.

'Answer the captain, lad,' growled Art, bounding into view with a sack slung over his shoulder.

'Captain?' whispered David. He must be dreaming. This couldn't be happening to him.

But why did he have to be so feeble even in his nightmares?

'Captain Reuben Fisher,' said the man, sweeping his hat off and making a low bow. 'At your service—though I hope your sudden arrival here uninvited means that you will soon be at mine?'

'Uninvited? You're joking. They made me come!'

'I think you'll find the technical term is "press-ganged"—quite within the rules of the sea,' continued Captain Fisher, 'though I don't like taking shipmates on board quite so young.' He turned David's face to the moonlight and drew a sharp intake of breath. 'There's something mighty familiar about you. Have you been to sea before, boy?'

David mutely shook his head.

'He saw us, I suppose?' the captain asked Art.

The monkey-fellow nodded.

'Then you had no choice. Still, I'm not sure about this one.'

'But, Captain, he knows about us now. We can't let him go,' argued Art.

Fisher grimaced. 'I suppose not. You're right as always. So, answer quickly, boy: what'll it be?'

'I . . . I don't understand,' mumbled David, wondering if he could run for it; but that snake-thing, Halist, was curled between him and the rail.

'Fish—shall we throw you overboard; fowl—shall we shut you up in a coop; or friend—shall we enter your name in the ship's log and give you your ration of grog like the rest of us?' Fisher folded his arms across his chest waiting for a response.

'Um . . . '

Captain Fisher smiled, an expression that made David even more nervous. 'Come, come, boy, you needn't take so long about it. There's no choice really.'

'Friend then,' said David grumpily.

The captain hauled David to his feet and clapped him on the shoulder. 'Welcome aboard the *Golden Needle*, shipmate.'

CHAPTER THREE
The Seas In-Between

David stood at the captain's side, still believing himself to be in a dream. Captain Fisher, satisfied that he had done all that was necessary with his newest recruit, turned his attention to the urgent matter of getting a three-masted square-rigger out of its berth in the back gardens of Waterside Row.

'Weigh anchor there!' he shouted to the men down at the stern. Well, 'men' was not the right description as they were as strange to David's eyes as Art and Halist, but he had no other suitable word for the members of this bizarre crew. The three sailors, one tall and spindly with four arms, his companions short with webbed hands and feet, started to crank up the heavy rope holding the anchor. Art untied the line securing the ship to David's conservatory roof and leapt nimbly back on board, moving swiftly using both hands and feet to propel himself along. When he spotted David watching him, he grinned, displaying a mouthful of sharp teeth.

'Hoist the mainsail,' cried Captain Fisher.

More members of the crew scuttled out of the hatchway from below decks like ants from a nest. They scurried up the three masts to take up position on the yardarms and let loose the furled canvas. As the sails tumbled down from their fastenings, David saw that they were made up of multicoloured scraps of cloth, the original white canvas now hardly to be seen after numerous repairs. Art sprang up the mainmast, heading for the crow's nest with a telescope tucked under one arm. The nest gleamed above the deck with a silvery light as if a star had come to roost there.

Captain Fisher sniffed the air.

'A fair breeze,' he commented approvingly, 'we'll make up some of the time we've lost.'

The sails bulged as they caught the wind, straining against the rigging. The masts creaked. Slowly the ship began to move.

How could this be happening? David wondered. A ship sailing on grass, that was impossible. Of the two, he preferred the latter explanation. He moved to the side and looked over: the grass shimmered in the starlight, wavering as if under water. Even Mrs Gordon's fence was undulating gently like seaweed, passing under the hull as if the obstruction could be merely brushed aside. David looked about him. Now the ship was sliding silently through the streets of Waterside like the boats on their passage through a Norwegian fjord. A seagull circled the mainmast and mewed plaintively before settling on the aerial of number thirty-three. David could feel the wind on his face and the spray of water whipping back from the prow. He could taste salt on his lips.

It had to be a dream. It had to. Any moment now he would wake up in his bedroom and laugh about it.

But the other dreams had not been like this, a voice in his head cautioned. There was no feel of breeze, no touch of spray, no sound of the singing of the ship's ropes in his dreams. No strange sailors had manned the *Golden Needle*; he had had the deck to himself.

Then, if this were real, he had to get off before it carried him too far from his home.

No sooner had he had this thought than the houses began to fade and the grass was replaced by water as if a flood had bubbled up during those few seconds and drowned the world he knew. Looking back, Waterside was lost as a fog-bank rolled in, hiding the houses, fences, trees, and cars. The sun was getting stronger, though surely it could not yet be morning? He could feel it beating on his back as he stared into the fog. Turning round, he saw to the right, or starboard, a turquoise blue sky above a sparkling ocean that seemed to stretch in all directions, twinkling and winking with promise.

This couldn't be right: his house was nowhere near the sea. *I am going mad!* he decided. He wanted to be at home, not standing in his pyjamas on a sun-drenched deck surrounded by strange crea-tures. His brain felt it would explode with the overload of impossible things that he was seeing.

Get a grip, David, he told himself. *You're a rational being, rational enough to know that this is completely mental. So therefore you're not mad. I hope. Sleep's the answer. When you wake up you can bet that things will be back to normal.*

Finding that none of the crew was paying him any attention, David sought out a sunny corner by the prow, nestled in a coil of rope, feet slung comfortably over the edge, and settled himself down. Yes, sleep: it would be like a door opening back on to normality.

After counting sheep, reciting the names of all the rivers he could remember, and then trying not

to think of anything at all, David finally suc-
cumbed, lulled into forgetfulness by the creak of
the timbers and the hum of the wind in the rigging.

He had no dreams.

The noise of flapping in his ears and the feel of
rough rope scratching his legs woke him up.
Opening his eyes a crack, he saw above him the jib
fluttering loosely in the slackened breeze. In the
centre of the triangular sail was a familiar red
cross: his England team duvet cover waved jaunti-
ly at him, as if it thoroughly approved of the tran-
sition from bed to ship. Just above it, David
recognized the lost scrap of white cloth he had cut
out the previous day to make a sail for his model,
now patching a circular tear like a bullet hole.

The deck creaked as someone came to stand
behind him.

'Good to be flying the old flag again,' said
Captain Fisher. 'I am grateful for your donation.
Trust me: our need was greater than yours and
we've already lost too much time.'

David said nothing. He could not believe that
he was still here.

'Taciturn chap, aren't you, boy?' commented
Captain Fisher. 'Well, look lively. I want you
down in my cabin—at the double.'

Despite his bewildered state of mind, David knew what was due the captain of any ship— even a dream one. He jumped to his feet and followed Fisher as he strode across the deck towards his quarters. The ship dipped into a trough in the waves and David staggered, unused to the motion of the sea. Art, who was now sitting cross-legged on the capstan sewing a flag, laughed. David shot him an angry look.

'Look, I haven't done this before!' he snapped.

'Don't mind him,' said Captain Fisher as he flung his hat onto the table in the centre of his cabin. 'He finds all us humans awkward beasts. Carlians are a surly bunch. But he's the best hand on the rigging, as I expect you saw. Worth his weight in gold to a ship is Artimage Simkindel.'

David stood to attention in his bare feet, hands clasped behind his back, wondering what was going to happen to him. Perhaps he was ill. Perhaps this was all some kind of hallucination and he would wake up in hospital in a few days' time?

'Strange you came to us, boy,' mused Captain Fisher as he sank into his chair behind the table.

David stared down at his toes. Instinct told him that if he met the captain's eye he would be a step nearer to admitting that this was somehow real. Fisher felt too vibrant, too alive to be a figment of his imagination.

'Not sure I like the look of you,' the captain continued.

And do dreams make a habit of insulting you? That didn't seem fair.

David shrugged, thinking it wasn't his fault if his face didn't please. He'd not asked to be here.

'Answer "Aye, aye, Captain" or "No, sir" when I ask you a question,' said Fisher sternly.

'Aye, aye, Captain,' said David quickly.

'So, why you, eh? That's what I'd like to know. Many of us are here paying for our past but I can't imagine you've done anything in your short life to deserve that.'

The captain didn't appear to expect an answer, so David remained silent. His gaze took in the three glazed windows behind the captain's desk. Their thick glass gave a blurred view of the sea they had just sailed through. The wake glinted with two lines of gold. The cabin itself was spacious and neatly furnished. Every corner seemed to contain something that David wished he owned. A collection of model ships had been tacked to the walls—Chinese junks, men-o'-war, cutters, sloops, and many others that David could not name. Gleaming gold instruments—sextants, compasses, clocks—were fastened to shelves either side of the cabin. A magnificent brass telescope stood by the window. The teak desk was covered with charts, criss-crossed with tiny golden lines. In the centre, a large rounded object huddled underneath a black velvet cloth, doubtless some other treasure of the navigator's art. To starboard was a narrow bunk with a blue satin cover embroidered with a compass. To the left, or port, was a gilded cage. Inside, an ancient-looking grey parrot glared back at him.

Perhaps he'd pass on owning the bird.

'What do you think, Jemima?' the captain asked. David realized that he was talking to the parrot.

'Running away! Running away!' she squawked.

'Is that so? You're running away from something, son?'

David was on the point of saying something rude about being forced on board, but then he remembered the brig, the place for unruly crew members.

'No, sir.'

'Well, there must have been some reason. You would never have seen us if there wasn't. And no one else could have made this.'

The captain lifted the black cloth with a flourish, revealing David's ship in a bottle.

'That's mine!'

Fisher tapped the bottle. 'Actually, I've merely borrowed it on permanent loan.'

David crossed his arms. 'Actually, the technical term is "stolen".'

The captain laughed. 'Where I come from, possession is nine-tenths of the law. But the question is, how did you of all people come to make it?'

David sensed that he and his model had permanently parted company. 'I saw it in my dreams, sir,' he replied sullenly.

'Exactly. But why? Beautiful, isn't she?' The captain stroked the glass. 'You must feel it, too, having made this. Oh, I know there's not a spar left from the original, but the lines are still the same, those elegant lines from stem to stern, a hull that cuts through the waves like a well-sharpened plough. The sails are a patchwork, I admit, but they still sing in the wind as they used to on the Spanish Main. She's the same lady to me, even if she's changed her name.' The captain turned his eyes on David. 'What's your name, boy?'

'David Jones.'

Captain Fisher picked up a scroll from his desk, sucked his teeth and tapped the roll of paper against his cheek thoughtfully.

'Thought as much,' he said softly to himself. 'His blood in you, if your face speaks the truth. But what's a Jones doing on my ship?'

Then, coming back to the business at hand, he took out a thick black book from his desk drawer, banged it down on the table and dipped a quill in the inkwell.

'Well, David Jones, sign here. Art, my first mate, will explain the ship's rules to our newest cabin boy. But know this before you step one foot outside: my word is law. Disobey it and I can have you strung from the yardarm. Obey me, and you'll earn your reward.'

'Reward?' asked David, the quill quivering in his hand. A droplet of black ink beaded at the point ready to fall on the paper.

The captain pushed his chair away from the table and paced to his window, looking out on the sparkling waters.

'For most of us our reward is to be clear of our debts, to be truly free. For you? I don't know what yours is yet. Perhaps only you can find that out.' He turned to grin at David. 'Let me know when you've worked it out. But you'll find we all have something twisted—twisted like a rope—inside us. Most of us are here to *unwind*.'

He laughed as if he had said something funny. David gave a confused smile, enough to prove that he too had a sense of humour, and signed his name in the book.

'Off you go, lad. I need to check the charts.'

With a flick of his wrist, Captain Fisher dismissed him.

36

David supposed he should seek out the first mate, but he did not much fancy meeting the monkey-man just then. He had far too much on his mind to listen to a lecture on rules. Instead, he climbed to the poop deck, the high platform at the rear of the ship where the wheel was found. As he mounted the steps, a school of flying fish, silver bright, flashed in the bow wave. A blue-grey dolphin leapt in a graceful arc out of the water before plunging back down into the depths again.

'Wow!' he exclaimed softly, gripped by wild joy at the sight, his sense of adventure stirred. 'This place is amazing.' But where exactly was he? And what ocean was this?

Looking to starboard, he saw a smoky haze on the horizon. It didn't look like land: more like a dark cloud. Even as he watched, he felt the ship change course, bringing her prow to race towards the darkness.

A whisper of wind in his ear and David found his lobe being pulled by a slim, pale, green-skinned hand.

'Ahoy there, Cabin Boy, thinking of turning me out of my job, are you?' The voice was clear and high.

David was about to slap the hand away but stopped. The little child to whom it belonged looked too frail for such treatment. She was about the size of David's three-year-old cousin, but much slighter and pretty in her own elfin way. Her skin had a hue like the green flush on the snowdrop as it nears the stem. Her long curling hair was the colour of the flying fish he had just been admiring. It blew in a cloud around her thin, angular face. But her eyes—her eyes were not so delicate—dark blue splinters of ice glittering with mischief. She seemed to glow even in the daylight with a cold, silvery light. David remembered the glimmer he had seen in the crow's nest when they set sail. Had that been her?

'What job?' asked David. 'I don't understand what you're going on about.'

The silver-green girl laughed, the jagged notes tinkling in the air.

'No, you wouldn't. I'm Shushula, cabin girl of the *Golden Needle*.'

'Oh,' said David. He hadn't realized that his arrival would offend anyone. 'I don't want to take anything from anyone—'

'You'd be the first to say that in this crew,' interrupted Shushula, nodding at the duvet cover fluttering down on the prow.

'All I want to do is wake up,' finished David.

'Wake up? But you *have* woken up—this is what you've been blind to all your life. You've been like a sleepwalker.'

David wanted to tell her not to be so stupid. His situation was only bearable if he thought it all one elaborate dream. But the wind was in his hair, the planks hot beneath his bare toes, his stomach rumbling to demand its breakfast. It was too real to be a dream; he was too 'here' to dismiss it as a phantom. He shook his head to deny what she was saying, but his heart had become strangely rebellious and was agreeing with her.

Shushula gave him a knowing smile. 'Uncanny, isn't it? I thought so too when the crew rescued me from my home on Tintel.' Her bright face clouded for a moment like a cloud passing over the moon. 'I found you humans really frightening to begin with—so clumsy! I was afraid every moment that I was going to be crushed by the captain's big boots. At least you don't have those.' She looked approvingly at his toes wriggling on the top step. 'But you'll get used to the *Needle*. Now, I don't want to be anywhere else.'

David looked at her earnest face and gave in. It made no sense to hold out that this was all a dream when it felt more real than most ordinary days at home.

'So where are we?' he asked, slumping down beside her. When seated, his head was on a level with hers.

'We're sailing the Seas In-between.' She leant over the side and looked out over the ever-moving surface.

'In-between what?'

'In-between the worlds, of course, you landlubber.'

Her explanations only raised more questions in David's mind.

'What worlds?'

'Your world, my world, all the known worlds—and probably many that are unknown too.' David still looked confused so she continued. 'The captain once showed me a book from Earth. It had a picture where if you looked at it one way it was a candlestick; the other, two faces.'

David nodded, remembering an optical illusion he had once seen. 'I know the kind of thing you mean.'

'Well, it's a bit like that out here. There's another way of seeing, different from what you think you know. Here, the worlds do not spin in empty space but drift on an endless sea. Since the beginning of time, they've been slowly moving apart on the currents, but it's happening much faster now. That is why we were sent here, of course.'

None of this yet made sense: an infinite sea, worlds drifting like rudderless ships. It was too much to take in.

'What worlds are you talking about?' he asked, hoping he didn't sound too thick.

She rubbed her nose thoughtfully. 'Well, for a start, there's Earth and Carl—we go to those worlds quite a lot as they are good for scavenging. Then, there's Scaranga and West Tiberg; Tarnis, Cho, and Dam—but we don't go there unless we must—horrid place.'

'And what about Tintel?' asked David, remembering the name she had given her home.

'We can't reach Tintel any more,' she said, her voice tight. 'It's gone beyond our reach into the Inferno Rim.'

'Inferno Rim?' David asked cautiously. He sensed that the subject was painful to her.

She nodded. 'Yes, the fiery waters that surround the Seas In-between. Your world is at their edge, as you can see from the sun above us.'

David did not have to look for he could feel the sun hot on the back of his neck.

'So, if the Inferno Rim is at the edge, what's at the centre?'

'Ah.' Shushula gave a mysterious smile. 'We've never reached it, but the captain says that, as you sail into the heart of the Seas In-between, the stars take over from the sun and it's always night. You live slower on the Seas In-between, you know. And if you keep on sailing, you reach a point where time stands still altogether and you can rest in an eternal moment, bathed in the light of the stars. You find perfect peace and rest from all sorrow.' She sighed. 'We sail under the starlight often enough, but we've never gone to the centre. We skirt round it, making great voyages across the seas. The captain says we're not ready to go there yet—not, at least, until we've finished our task and earned the rest.'

'What task is that?'

Shushula poked him playfully. 'Is there no end to your questions, Human?'

'Actually, I'm called David.'

Shushula pulled him to his feet with her cool hands. 'Come, I'll show you, David.'

She ran nimbly past the wheel, manned for the moment by an unsmiling Art, to the stern. Beckoning to David, she pointed to the water behind the ship. There he saw clearly what he had only glimpsed from the captain's windows: behind the ship stretched two long, thin ropes made of gold.

'See, the *Golden Needle* is drawing her thread,' said Shushula, pointing to a vast reel of the same material unwinding from the stern rail.

'What is she sewing?' asked David in amazement.

'She's sewing the worlds together, of course. That's why she was brought here with her crew— to stop the worlds sailing too far apart. Only gold will serve for the thread. We take the cord to each world, secure it there, then sail on to the next port, binding them together with our stitch. There used to be thousands of threads criss-crossing the ocean.'

'But how can that possibly work? What happens if the threads snap or are cut?' David asked.

'The worlds will drift off into the Inferno Rim. Their life fades and we can no longer visit them. The secret ports made in each world are closed to us.'

'Is that what happened to Tintel?'

She nodded, her eyes glistening with tears, but she wiped them roughly away. 'Everyone's gone. I'm the only one left. It's so . . . lonely.'

That simple word sank between them, weighed down with unbearable sadness.

'And my world?' David asked fearfully.

'Your world is safe—for the present. Captain Fisher has no desire to let his home slip from under his fingers. He'll do his best to save it. But he tried hard for Tintel too, so . . . ' She shrugged, leaving him to guess the rest.

'So the Earth is doomed?'

'Only if we fail.'

'Oh, that's all right then.' A bunch of gold threads didn't sound very much to stand between the Earth and disaster.

She seemed to be reading his mind. 'The thread is very strong—specially woven.'

'I'm pleased to hear it.'

'It might never happen.'

'I s'pose not.'

She gave up trying to reassure him and changed the subject. 'Well, David, you must be hungry. Shall we see what foul mess Halist has cooked up for us?'

David nodded. A bell sounded once down on the main deck.

'It's gone noon,' he said, remembering how hungry he was.

'So, you're not completely ignorant, I see,' Shushula said, giving him an approving look. 'Last one to the galley is a squid!'

With that, she ran lightly back to the poop deck stairs, David knowing that he was destined to lose even before he set off in pursuit.

CHAPTER FOUR
Sea Battle

When David arrived down on the main deck he found most of the crew gathered by the hatch to the kitchen. On the counter lay a steaming black cauldron. Halist reared up behind it with a ladle grasped in his fangs, hissing as loudly as the bubbling mixture he was about to serve.

'What's it today?' called out a tall creature with blue skin at the front of the queue.

Halist, of course, could not answer as his mouth was currently occupied in spooning the green gloop into a wooden bowl.

'Smells like gartan stew,' sniffed the second creature in the queue, a stubby fellow with short legs and a squashed nose like a pig.

'What!' protested the first speaker. 'Not again! We had that yesterday.'

'And the day before that, and the day before that,' added Shushula under her breath to David.

Halist glared at them all and shoved the first bowl to the edge of the hatch, clearly intending to push it right over if no one took it. Reluctantly, the blue-skinned sailor seized it and strode off to find a place to eat. The queue continued to move unenthusiastically to the hatch. When it came to David's turn, he picked up his bowl and wooden spoon with a murmur of thanks and followed Shushula to the capstan. They sat on top, legs crossed, with their bowls cradled in their laps.

'Go on,' said Shushula mischievously. 'Try it.'

David sniffed the steam curling up from the jellified mess: it smelt like petrol. He noticed that she hadn't risked it yet.

'What is it?' he asked uncertainly, letting a spoonful drip back into the bowl. It quivered in the bottom.

'Gartan. A fruit from Carl. And yes: it does taste as bad as it smells. Only the first mate likes it.' This seemed to be true because Art was spooning great mouthfuls down eagerly not far from them, while cracking jokes with the morose blue-skinned sailor. Shushula gingerly sipped a little of the stew and wrinkled her nose in disgust.

'Fortunately, I don't need to eat much to stay alive.' She put her spoon down. 'But you humans do, don't you? Go on: it's all there is.'

Not wishing to appear a coward over so small a thing, David held his nose and took the plunge. A bitter taste filled his mouth. He coughed. He retched. It was truly the most revolting thing he had ever tasted, even worse than chewing an aspirin.

Shushula laughed. 'Oh, you'll get used to it. You'll eat it if you're hungry enough.'

David put his bowl to one side. He wasn't hungry enough—not yet.

'So who are you all?' he asked Shushula, looking around at the motley band of creatures dining in the waning light. It wasn't that it was getting late, he realized, it was just that they were approaching the darkness he had seen on the horizon earlier that day. The starlit seas, the dark waters at the heart of the Seas In-between, were near.

'Who are we?' repeated Shushula. Her hair fluttered over her face, glinting like spiderwebs caught in autumn sunshine. 'We're like you: we're here because we have to be.'

That didn't tell him much so David tried a more specific question.

'What about the captain? He's from my world, you say, but I've never met anyone like him before. No one I know dresses like that.'

47

'Really?' said Shushula with interest. 'Earth changes a lot, doesn't it? I've noticed that even during the short visits I've paid to it. Well, things change there swiftly compared to on the Seas In-between. We live slower here—much slower. Captain Fisher left your world hundreds of your years ago.'

'No?' said David incredulously. 'But that means . . . '

'It means that he is old, very old, by your reckoning. He was a pirate.' Shushula spat as she said the word.

'A pirate?'

'Yes, one of the worst, by all accounts. Happy to maroon a man just for looking at him in a way he did not like. Careless of the lives he lost in going after gold. He's got many years of work ahead to pay back his debt, he says.'

David hugged his knees. Captain Fisher had said many were here serving some kind of sentence. Did that mean that he—David—had been bad too?

'So you're a bunch of criminals?'

Shushula shook her head. 'We're not all bad on the *Golden Needle*. To choose to be here shows that you are pure at heart, ready to make amends. Some of us are just here to escape—not because we did anything wrong. If someone's rotten at the core, they'd be with the pirates on the *Scythe*.'

'Who are they?'

'They're led by Captain Fisher's greatest ene-my—an evil man. His ship—the *Scythe*—chases us relentlessly, cutting the thread to steal the gold.'

David felt sickened as he thought of the threads binding the worlds together being sev-ered in this way.

'Don't they care about the damage they do?'

Shushula laughed darkly. 'Not them. So, David, why are you here?'

David frowned. Why was he here?

'The captain asked me the same question. I don't know.'

'Were you happy at home?'

When David thought of his family, the tiger-pain he had been hunted by for so long came back and bit hard. Now he had the added worry of what his mother would think when she found him gone.

'Sort of,' he said finally. 'I love my mum—and my grandad.'

'But?' probed the girl gently.

'Dad left us.'

'I see.'

And David felt that she did. He looked up at her sad face and recognized that she knew what it was like to lose someone. The pain eased a little like the loosening of the first knots in a tangle.

David looked the way they had come, back to home. Something twinkled white on the horizon.

'What's that?' he asked, tapping Shushula's arm to draw her attention. Shushula jumped up, shading her eyes against the glare. Her body went rigid.

'Pirates!' she hissed under her breath. Then to the rest of the crew she shouted: 'Sail ahoy!'

Suddenly, everyone leapt up, stew flew in all directions, spoons clattered to the deck.

'Where?' growled Art, clambering up the nearest rope.

'Portside,' Shushula replied. 'Is it the *Scythe*?'

Art took a telescope from his waistband and trained it on the distant sail.

'It is,' he confirmed, shutting the telescope with a snap. 'Battle stations! Clear the decks! Summon the captain.'

A drum began to beat somewhere below decks. David found himself in the middle of a whirlwind of running feet, jostling bodies, and shouting crewmen. He watched, feeling completely useless, as the crew prepared to fight. The bowls were swept away. Brushes and buckets stowed. The guns were run out.

'Get off of there, laddie,' bellowed Art when he saw David sitting on the capstan. 'You'll be a prime target for a musket shot if you stay up there.'

David slid down quickly.

Art gave him a second look, taking in the boy's bewildered expression.

'Here, lad, you can be my powder monkey,' said the first mate, thrusting a funnel-shaped horn into his hands. 'Get below and fill this for me.'

Below decks, the hammocks had been taken down and the wooden partitions cleared so that the gunners had a space to do their work. David followed Shushula's silver light to the powder magazine where Halist was doling out black gunpowder.

'Tastes better than his cooking,' whispered Shushula with a grin as she turned to leave. He was amazed she could make jokes at such a time, but he supposed she must be hardened to battles by now.

Back on deck, David found Art talking to Captain Fisher.

'I don't know how he's doing it, Captain,' said Art in a low voice. 'We've packed on all the sail we can manage and he's still catching up with us. We used to outrun the *Scythe* easily.'

'Aye,' said Fisher, 'something's changed all right. Well, we have no choice now but to fight, hope we damage him more than he does us, and then make a run for it.'

Art grunted his agreement. 'At least we have the advantage that we don't care if we sink his ship. He won't want to let our golden thread go to the bottom if he can help it.'

'True. Gold was always Captain Tiberius's undoing.'

The captain strode away to check that the rest of his crew was ready for battle. Art piled up his shot, helped by the blue-skinned man David had noticed earlier.

'All set, lad?' said Art when he saw David. 'Got the powder?'

'Aye, sir,' said David, holding the horn out with a trembling hand. He was annoyed that his body was betraying his fear to all these professional seamen. He would have liked to be bolder and braver but, to be honest, he felt scared stiff. He had heard enough about sea battles from his grandad to know that they were ugly affairs, leading to blood on the deck, amputations by rough surgeons, and burials at sea stitched up in your hammock. He could now see the enemy ship quite clearly. It had three masts all straining with yellow, patched canvas. Its hull was painted black and gold and glittered dully in the sunlight. The distance between them was rapidly closing and he could make out the figurehead carved in the shape of a Grim Reaper bearing a scythe.

The prow was very odd: it was sharp-nosed and clad in iron. *To cut the thread,* David realized with a shudder. Whatever else the prow was designed to do, one thing was for certain: it was bearing down on them with astonishing speed. A black cloud followed in the ship's wake, haunted by the flitting shapes of many seabirds.

'They're after the fish,' said Art calmly as he took the horn and tipped some of its contents into a quill to insert into the gunlock.

'Fish?'

'Yes. The sea hates the *Scythe* so much these days that fish die in their hundreds as it passes over. The seabirds know this but the fish they gorge on do them no good. Many of them die in agony a few days after the feast. Uncanny, I think.'

David agreed with him but said nothing as he could tell that Art was concentrating on his task of preparing the cannon.

'Been in battle before, lad?' asked Art when he'd finished priming the gun.

David shook his head.

'Well, keep your head down when the splinters start to fly. The *Scythe* hardly used to bother us; nowadays we need more and more repairs—both men and ship—after the battle. The *Golden Needle* is now only a shadow of her former self.

That's why the captain wanted your little ship when Shushula told him of it—a sentimental gesture, something to remember her glory days by, he said.'

There was a crack from the prow of the *Scythe*, followed by a whistle. A small round object splashed into the water well short of the stern of the *Golden Needle*.

'You'll have to do better than that,' chuckled Art. 'No good using your swivel guns on us, matey.'

'What are they doing?' asked David anxiously.

'Probably trying to crack one of the captain's windows out of spite,' said Art. 'Tiberius Jones hates his guts. But you needn't worry until they come alongside to give us a broadside.'

The guns crackled again. This time David saw a spray of holes open up in one of the sails.

'Wait for it—wait for the order!' he heard Captain Fisher shout. 'Swivel guns we can weather. We have the wind in our favour. We make our pass then head for the darkness so you'll have just one chance, lads, to wing him.'

'Aye, aye, Captain!' cheered the crew in unison.

David felt his heartbeat pick up pace with excitement. He was frightened, very frightened, but somehow being among an experienced crew gave him a new confidence. They'd do their best—he'd do his best—and that was all that could be expected of any of them.

He glanced to his right to the next gun. Shushula was standing behind it next to a tall, female sailor, dressed in a pristine white shirt and breeches. But the most remarkable thing about this sailor was that her skin was striped like a tiger and when she turned towards him, he saw that she had the chilling stare of a cat.

'Who's that?' he asked Art.

Art gave a careless glance to one side.

'Ruramina—a West Tibergian and our second mate. A fine sailor. Now, lad, keep your eyes on the enemy—we're almost there.'

The captain's voice sliced through the air shouting an order to cut across the path of the *Scythe*. Briskly the ship changed direction, steering on a collision course, it seemed to David, with the enemy. The two ships were now so close that he could see a broad-shouldered man in a plumed hat at the prow, a musket on his shoulder prepared to fire.

Up on the poop deck of the *Golden Needle*, Captain Fisher swept his own hat from his head and bowed low.

'Captain Jones, a pleasure as always,' he bellowed across the narrowing strait of water between them. 'But why not come aboard for a drink to old times rather than meet me in this warlike manner?'

His answer was a crack from the musket and the rail near Captain Fisher splintered where the ball struck it.

'Gunners!' roared the captain, jumping nimbly down to the main deck.

The *Scythe* came in range of a broadside. The cannons rang out. David's head echoed with the din. Ropes flew apart in the rigging of the pirate vessel; the main yardarm hung limp like a broken wing. A sail tumbled down to the deck, burying some crew members underneath.

'Why haven't they fired back?' shouted David when his hearing had been restored.

Art was busy with his companion reloading the gun.

'Can't till he gets alongside. Won't be able to get his cannons to bear on us until they turn and, if the captain has his way, we'll be long gone before then.'

The *Golden Needle* was tacking to pass in front of the *Scythe* again. Art looked up with concern. They could now all hear a loud throbbing noise coming from the other ship. The *Scythe* picked up its speed.

'Crab's claws!' cursed Art. 'We'll not make a second pass. They'll be alongside before we can do our turn. Batten down the hatches, boy!'

David could see what he meant. The *Scythe* was catching them up halfway through the man-oeuvre so that she could bring her guns into range. The port side blossomed with one puff of smoke after another, rapidly followed by a loud report. The guns on the *Golden Needle* that had managed to reload answered, blowing holes in the black hull of the pirate ship. On board the *Golden Needle*, as the attack hit home, wood splinters flew in the air. Ropes fell to the deck, coiling like snakes as they came. David covered his head with his hands and felt a splinter nick his arm.

'They're shooting high,' growled Art, looking up at the rigging. 'They want to take us as a prize—not sink us. Watch out for the muskets, lad.'

Captain Fisher could be heard cursing his bad fortune.

'Dammit! Jones must have the devil on his side. Run for the shadows!' he called out to the man at the wheel.

The ship creaked as the rudder took hold, steering them towards the darkness that was now at hand. Shadows deepened on the deck; David felt the air begin to chill. But they had not moved quickly enough to be out of range of a second barrage from the *Scythe*. Angry orange flared at the mouth of each gun like dragon-fire and the shots fell lower this time. Many things happened all at once. The rail between David's gun and Shushula's was blown completely away. Timber flew into the air. Art seized David and threw himself on top of the boy to protect him from the splinters now raining upon them. David didn't dare move. He could feel the rough pelt of the Carlian on his face, hear his heart beating almost as loudly as his own, smell the odour of sweat and powder that the whole gun crew now shared. Then Art heaved himself off David, clutching the back of his head. The ship was in total darkness.

'Silence—no lights—Shushula below,' came the captain's voice, soft so that only his crew could hear.

A faint silvery gleam moved to his right and David guessed that Shushula was obeying the order. It was good to know that she had survived. He wished he could thank Art for protecting him but the Carlian was busy about the gun. David didn't know what to do. He felt a tap on his shoulder.

'Below!' murmured the captain.

David stumbled after him to the stern and into the captain's cabin. Captain Fisher went to the windows and fumbled about in the dark to pull some heavy velvet drapes across the glass. Only when every chink had been covered did he strike a match to light a lantern.

'You'll find, Davy Jones, that it's part of a cabin boy's duties to look after his captain's welfare,' he said softly as he hung the lantern from a hook in the ceiling. It swayed gently in time with the swell.

'Sir?' said David.

'I've taken a nick and need you to bind it for me,' the captain explained. He unbound a scarf at his neck to reveal a nasty cut which was bleeding into the hairs on his chest. 'Hurry, lad, before it spoils my best shirt.'

David glanced around him. His eyes lighted on a jug of water, basin, and linen towel by the bed. He wetted the cloth and hurried back to Fisher.

'You did well, lad!' the captain said as David gently wiped away the blood. 'You kept your head under fire. Many first timers can't say as much.'

David felt pleased to receive this praise but modestly said nothing as he wrung out the cloth. He returned to clean the wound itself.

'Ouch!' The captain flinched as the wound stung under David's hand. 'It's bad enough having my chest sliced open by Tiberius without having his kinsman make it worse!' His voice was good-humoured but David sensed that there was real anger underneath.

'Kinsman?' David asked. 'But I don't . . . I'm not—'

'Aye, that you are, lad,' said Captain Fisher, brushing the cloth away. 'I knew it the moment I set eyes on you. It's not your fault, I know. None of us can help our relations. But why did fate bring you to us, eh? Why not to him?'

David was still reeling from the accusation— for that was how it felt—that he was related to the captain of the ship that had just tried to kill him.

'But I don't have a relation called T-Tiberius,' he stuttered.

'Don't now, maybe, but you did once. You are the exact image of him as a boy—I should know for we served together as youngsters. That was before I became captain, of course. I saw the resemblance the moment I had a proper look at you. Wanted to throw you straight over the side—would've done in the old days—but it seems that destiny has brought you to us and I have to put up with a vision of my wicked past haunting my cabin. Perhaps it's all part of my mending,' he mused, rubbing his bristly chin.

Could this be true? David asked himself. Could he have a pirate for an ancestor? His grandad had once said that he came from a family of seafarers but David had always thought him to mean the

Royal Navy. And Jones was a very common name.

'I don't believe it. Sir,' he added quickly when he saw the anger glisten in Captain Fisher's eyes.

'You'd better believe it, boy. I haven't lived for three hundred years without learning a thing or two and I know a Jones when I see one.'

There was a knock at the door.

'Come!' barked the captain.

Art and the tall tiger woman, Ruramina, entered, shutting the door quickly behind them. Art had a bloodied bandage around his scalp.

'Report?'

'As far as we can tell, Captain, without light, we've sustained most damage to the starboard rail and stern mast. We're taking in water, but nothing the pumps can't handle,' said Art.

This appeared to be good news for the captain smiled.

'How did he do it, sir?' asked Ruramina. Her voice was deep and silky—almost a purr. Her tail twitched angrily to and fro.

'I don't know, I don't know,' said the captain, shaking his head. 'He's got hold of something that gives him the advantage of us. If we don't find out what it is very quickly, I fear that we will fail in our task. Already many of the worlds are drifting apart faster than we can sew them together.'

'Aye,' grunted Art. 'There's evidence the *Scythe* isn't the only one at it. One of those threads we picked up from the water last week was cut on Carl. There's an enemy on land sabotaging our work.'

'Someone else who knows about us, someone not on one of the ships?' queried Fisher.

'Aye, sir.'

An ominous silence fell in the cabin. Ruramina licked her fingers thoughtfully.

'What we need is a spy,' she said at length. 'We need someone on the *Scythe* to find out what Jones is doing. He might be in league with this thread-cutter. At the very least, we need to find out the cause of the *Scythe*'s new capabilities.'

The captain sat forward in his chair.

'I think you're right. But how will we get someone on board? Are any of the crew good at concealment?'

Ruramina shook her head. 'I don't think concealment is the answer. We need to trick Captain Jones into taking someone on board gladly. Someone he does not know but has every reason to trust. Someone new to the Seas In-between.' David shuddered as he felt her eyes turn on him.

Art stirred restlessly. 'I understand you,' he growled, 'but I don't like it. It's too dangerous.'

Captain Fisher looked from Art to Ruramina and finally to David. With a heavy heart, David realized what they were thinking.

'What do you say, Davy?' asked the captain.

David looked at his feet, blackened with dirt. His pyjamas were ripped at the knees: his mother would be furious, he thought mechanically as his mind refused to answer the question posed to him.

'He doesn't know what is at stake,' purred Ruramina. 'If he did, he would do it for the sake of all of us.'

But he did know. Shushula had told him enough for him to understand that something terrible would happen to Earth if the *Golden Needle* failed in her task. He'd never be able to go home. And would they really give him any choice? Fisher was a formidable captain; he didn't fancy refusing an order from him. Better to accept the task willingly than have it thrust upon him, he thought.

'Captain, why don't you send me?' he said in a small voice.

Art grunted. He clearly hated this idea.

'If we pretend to maroon him, Captain Jones will think I'm punishing him,' said Captain Fisher, the elements of a plan slotting into place.

'But, Captain!' protested Art, limping forward. 'How'll the boy get back, even if he does succeed in getting on board safely?'

'You forget, Art, that the *Scythe* is looking for us. We'll never be far away. Can you swim, boy?'

'Sort of,' admitted David, though a length of the school pool had hardly prepared him for open sea.

'That's settled then: he can go overboard in the next encounter and we'll scoop him out of the drink.'

This sounded suspiciously easy. If the battle he had just lived through had taught David one thing, it was that you had to be prepared for the unexpected turn of fortune. And how would he fare in the heat of battle with cannon balls and musket shot raining down on the water?

'But, sir—' began Art.

Captain Fisher's mind was made up. 'Do you have a better idea, First Mate? If you do, I'd like to hear it.'

Art grunted but said nothing.

'Well, my boy, your noble offer is accepted.' Fisher held out his palm to the cabin boy, displaying once more the shark tattoo below his sleeve making as if to bite David's hand. 'Make the preparations, Ruramina.'

With a curt nod, Captain Fisher dismissed his crew. David staggered out of the cabin into the night. It was only when he took a gulp of the chilly air that it really struck him that, after being press-ganged into service and spending less than a day on board, he had now offered to be marooned. What had he been thinking?

CHAPTER FIVE
Marooned

Shushula was very excited when she heard what David had volunteered to do. She heard the news up in the crow's nest and immediately slipped down the nearest rope and landed on the deck in front of him.

'David, I just had to tell you: you're so brave!' she said admiringly.

'Bonkers, you mean,' he corrected, still feeling dazed by the fit of madness that had resulted in him offering to go on the mission.

'No, brave. Don't you go thinking otherwise.' She looked through the little bundle of provisions he had been given. David was pleased to see that the ship's biscuit looked more appetizing than the stew. 'They've not given you much, have they?'

'No. The captain said it would give the game away if I were too well stocked. I'm to bury even that when I see the *Scythe* arriving.' David felt someone else was speaking, talking so calmly about the adventure ahead. The real him was quivering inside.

Shushula nodded her head with understanding. 'Ah yes, in his old life, the captain would never've left a marooned man with any comforts.'

David grimaced. 'Not sure I like the sound of this captain of yours.'

'*Your* captain too, David.'

He shrugged; he hardly knew Fisher, certainly not well enough to feel any desire to pledge his loyalty to him. What did he know of the man but that he disliked David's face due to some unfortunate resemblance to an old enemy and that he was prepared to use him to discover the *Scythe*'s secret? Whatever way you looked at it, that was not very reassuring.

'You wouldn't feel like that if you realized what he was like,' continued Shushula, reading the doubt in his expression. 'He risked the ship coming to save me from Tintel. I was stranded on a melting ice floe and he rowed out in his launch himself to collect me despite the snow bears swarming everywhere. Not that I blame the bears for attacking; they were as desperate as me to escape the heat.'

'That sounds very . . . very brave of him.'

'Yes, he's courageous and loyal to his crew. He does his best to make up for his past. He's the first to admit that he was a vicious thug, but he's changed.'

'Has he?' David was eager for some proof that he wasn't a complete fool to trust his life to this man. 'How can you be sure?'

'Is three hundred years of sewing not enough?' Shushula tapped his arm. 'Not that I'm saying he's all good. He still has flashes of—' She paused.

'Of what?'

'Of his old self, I suppose. He gets very annoyed when it happens. Says it puts him back years before he can earn his right to pass on the captaincy to another.'

'You're telling me he wants to retire?' David could not imagine Fisher taking to a quiet life raising roses in some suburban garden.

'He wants to be free,' corrected Shushula.

The stars twinkled overhead in the dark vault of the sky. Everything seemed so peaceful as the waves, frosted with starlight, lapped at the sides of the ship.

'Lower the boat!' commanded Captain Fisher from the poop deck.

Six crewmen hoisted the launch and swung it out over the side. With a gentle splash, it hit the water.

'Ready, Davy?' asked the captain, putting his hand on the boy's shoulder.

David didn't feel ready. How could you ever be ready for the gamble he was about to take?

'Aye, sir,' he said in a hoarse voice.

'Over the side with you then. I'll row you to the island myself.'

David dropped his little bundle of provisions down into the boat. Shushula touched his arm.

'We'll come for you. Don't doubt us, will you, Cabin Boy?'

David shook his head. His throat was now too dry for words. Swinging his leg over the rail he slid down the rope ladder and into the boat, taking a seat in the bow. The vessel rocked as Captain Fisher jumped down after him and took the oars.

'Not far now, lad,' he said cheerfully. 'I've chosen a good little island for you. I'll leave you with a lantern and a store of fuel. All you need do is keep the light going and the *Scythe* will be upon you in no time like a moth to a candle flame. In case there's a hitch, we'll sail back this way same time tomorrow and see if you're still here. But I've no doubt they'll follow your light, not least because they'll be looking for us in this gloom.'

David wondered how he would know it was tomorrow in this sunless sea but didn't mention this out loud. As Shushula said, all he could do was trust in his shipmates.

'It's a brave thing you're doing for us, Davy,' continued Captain Fisher as he took efficient, even strokes with the oars. The blades glistened as they dipped into the water. 'I've been thinking that maybe this is why you were sent to us. What do you think?'

'Perhaps,' shrugged David.

Fisher frowned at his cabin boy's casual manner.

'I mean, maybe so, sir, but I don't really understand any of this.'

Captain Fisher nodded. 'Aye, I've been here more years than I can remember and even I don't understand it fully. The universe is more mysterious than any of us can imagine. In a blink of an eye, we slip from one way of looking at things to another—all of them as real as each other. Like those secret ports on our world, visible only to us dwellers on the Seas In-between.'

David's ears pricked up. He'd been wondering about them.

'I've noticed that they are only found in places where land meets water—but not all places. I started to make a map of them years ago but gave up long since. It's the same on the other worlds. It seems that there's a weakness—a seam—created where the elements meet and the *Golden Needle* can slip through, sewing the world to the Seas In-between. The Seas are the element on which the worlds float, but it's the threads that hold everything together. There is no greater task than to keep them bound to each other. If we don't, life on the worlds will fade as they wither under the sun.'

David considered Fisher's words. He had heard about his own world warming up and knew that scientists made dire predictions as to what that would do to the environment, so it wasn't so hard to imagine that this might be true for other places too. The devastation on an ice world such as Tintel must have been massive. It would be no picnic on Earth either by the sounds of it.

'How long do worlds have once they reach the Inferno Rim?' he asked.

'Not long—unless you like living in a waterless desert. Once the heat gets a grip, the whole thing spirals out of control. Much better to keep to the Seas In-between.'

'So how did you come to be a captain here, sir?'

'I was called.' Fisher shipped his oars.

David didn't feel in the mood for enigmatic answers. After all, he was about to risk his life for this man. 'Was does that mean? Who called you?'

'I'll only know for sure when I reach the still point in the middle of the starlit seas, but I have my suspicions.' Fisher gave a wary smile, perhaps conscious he was confessing too much.

David frowned, not finding the answer very illuminating.

'Or you could say my conscience prompted me to accept the position,' Fisher added, returning to his usual businesslike manner. 'I was sick of myself and knew it was change or be damned. I was lucky to be given the chance.'

The keel of the boat ground to a halt on a beach.

'This is where you get out, Davy,' said the captain, passing him his bundle. 'Don't be scared now. The frapgins won't come near the light.'

David stopped, one foot in the water, the other still in the boat.

'Frapgins?' He hadn't heard a whisper about those.

Captain Fisher cleared his throat. 'Er . . . yes. They're big crablike creatures found only in the starlit seas. Make good eating if you can catch them, but I wouldn't advise you to try. There's many a sailor who's lost a limb to the frapgins.'

'Lost a limb!' David pulled his foot quickly out of the water.

'But as I said,' said the captain, 'they won't come near the light.' He passed David a lantern.

'Here, put that on the beach and return for the wood.'

'Is there anything else you haven't told me?' he asked, a shade resentfully.

The captain laughed. 'You mean like the headless ghouls?'

'Headless ghouls!'

'Just joking. No, the frapgins are the only unfriendly creatures I know of in this part of the Seas In-between.'

David wasn't sure he appreciated the captain's sense of humour. After all, it wasn't Fisher who was going to be left alone on a dark beach with only a lantern for company.

He dumped his belongings on the sand and came back for the fuel.

'We will see you very soon, I hope, Davy!' called Captain Fisher as he pushed off from the shore. 'If it gets difficult, remember, you're down in the log. I never abandon a shipmate—not now.'

David watched as the boat was swallowed up by the night. Then, recalling the warning about the mysterious frapgins, he splashed out of the warm shallow water to his lamp. The single candle flame suddenly seemed very frail. What if a puff of wind blew it out? He'd be left in the dark with no means of lighting it again. He hurriedly built up a campfire, realizing that he would be unable to sleep as all his attention would be needed to keep his fire burning.

He began to pace the beach to keep awake. The sand was soft but now and again the soles of his feet hit on a larger object. He bent down and held up a handful to the lantern. It was like silver grit mixed up with tiny bright blue shells. His mother would like those, he thought, putting some of the shells in his pocket. He could make her a necklace from them—if he ever saw her again, that was.

After walking about for as long as he could, David returned to the campfire, threw on more wood and sat down. He was hungry now. Fumbling in the little sack Art had given him for the ship's biscuits, he came across an unexpected object. Right at the bottom was a lock of silver hair that shone faintly in his fist. It could only belong to one person. Seeing Shushula's gift was sweet and bitter—sweet because he found comfort in knowing she was thinking of him; bitter because it made him realize just how alone he was. He'd almost welcome eating a bowl of Halist's cooking to be back on the *Needle* with Shushula.

Well, at least now I'll never be completely in the dark even if I run out of firewood before I'm rescued, he thought. He wound the lock of hair up and put it in his pyjama pocket.

Time to eat. He pulled out a tough square of biscuit and took a bite, fearing the worst. It wasn't bad—a bit too much like cardboard perhaps, but a definite improvement on the stew.

Time crawled by and David's eyes itched with tiredness. He splashed a little of his precious water on the back of his neck, shivering as a cool breeze chilled his wet skin. He wondered what his classmates would be thinking by now. They must know that he'd gone missing. He fantasized a few scenes where Ricko broke down in tears in front of the head teacher and confessed to his bullying, went on bended knee to beg David's mother's forgiveness . . .

Fat chance. He'd probably be celebrating with his mates.

David turned his mind from his least favourite person to his own predicament. Would the *Scythe* come, as the captain had so confidently said? Until this moment, he hadn't even asked himself what Jones and his crew were like; he had only been concerned that he would not spend too long marooned. Now he wondered what he had let himself in for? Life on Captain Fisher's boat had been tough enough; what then would it be like on the *Scythe*?

Click, click.

David sat up abruptly. Above the regular heartbeat of the waves on the shore and the crackle of the fire, he was sure he had heard something.

Click, click-click, click.

There was something out there, moving about beyond the shadows. David's mind leapt to the frapgins. He picked up the lantern, took two paces forward and held it up. He caught a glimpse of something white, about the size of his hand, scuttling away. Well, if that was all they were, they did not look too bad. They were no bigger than crabs in his world.

Emboldened, David moved forward quickly, spreading the arc of his lamp as far as it could go.

Click, click, click.

He yelled and dropped the light.

The lantern shattered on a rock and the candle fell flame-first into the sand. In his panic, David felt blindly about for it and cut his hand on the broken glass before finding the stub half buried. The clicking noise was coming nearer. He dashed back to his campfire and threw himself down in a shaking heap beside it, grabbing a piece of driftwood as a makeshift club. The white thing he had glimpsed had been but the tip of a claw of the whole beast. His lantern had shown him a giant white crab crawling sideways up the shore, pincers raised. Two red saucerlike eyes had glared at him momentarily. Its pincers had been the size of chainsaws. This was the creature that was now approaching. Maybe there were more? He glanced fearfully over his shoulder, convinced he could hear clicking from that direction too. He stirred the fire, sending sparks flying up. How much wood did he have left? He looked fearfully at the bundle he had been given, realizing that he had been too generous earlier on and had been consuming his store far too fast. He gave a sob of fear but then regained control of himself. The last thing he needed now was a panic attack. He had to sit tight and wait. The frapgin was coming no closer. Captain Fisher had been right about the light. He had nothing to fear from it as long as he kept his head.

If time had crawled before, it now appeared to have stopped moving altogether as David sat staring into the heart of the fire hugging his knees. When Shushula had described how they lived slower on the Seas In-between, it had sounded an attractive idea; now David realized what a burden it could be.

He shivered, unable to shake the feeling that he had tiny frapgins crawling up and down his spine—the loathsome offspring of the monster he had glimpsed. He could hear a tinkling sound from over by the rock where he had dropped the lantern. It appeared that the frapgin was investigating the shards of glass. He hoped its enquiries would stop there.

Hours later, David jolted awake as his head dropped off his knees. He sat up quickly. Had he really been asleep? The fire was still going—he must have only dozed for a second. His eyes swam, now seeing another light out to sea. He rubbed them, thinking he was beginning to imagine things, but the light stayed. David jumped to his feet, showering the fire with sand. It hissed and sparked blue.

'Ahoy!' he shouted. Grabbing a burning branch, he began to wave it over his head. 'Ahoy there!'

He heard the sound of oars creaking in the rowlocks but no one answered.

'Over here—I'm stranded—help!'

He had no idea of the time. It could be tomorrow already and it might only be the *Golden Needle* coming back.

'It's me—it's David!' he yelled at the top of his voice.

A rowing boat appeared out of the night and ground to a stop on the beach. A new shout died in David's throat. Perhaps Captain Fisher had

not been joking about he██████████
for there, sitting on the rower's ████
a black cloak, was a hunched skele███
grey-skinned arms shipping the oars. ██
hollow black eyes stared at him, set in a sta██
looking face.

'Who are you?' rasped the man.

'I'm David,' he gabbled in his terror, 'I was cabin boy on the *Golden Needle*—but Captain Fisher marooned me.'

'What did you do, Cabin Boy?'

'I don't know—he just took against me,' said David lamely.

The rower picked up his oars again. 'In that case, Cabin Boy, I'll leave you to your punishment. It's not for me to interfere between a captain and his crew.' His laugh sounded rusty from lack of use.

'No, wait!' shrieked David, running to the water's edge to grasp the edge of the boat. The man brought an oar heavily down with a crack on his fingers. David yelped. 'I do remember!' he sobbed, wading out into the water. 'He cast me off because he found out I was related to Tiberius Jones!'

The man stopped rowing.

'You—a kinsman of Tiberius Jones?'

'Yes!' cried David desperately.

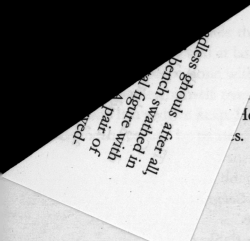

...an thought.
...I'll let the captain
...you.'

...the side of the boat
...He had managed it: he
...s.

80

CHAPTER SIX
The Scythe

T he skeletal man did not speak as he rowed across the short stretch of water that separated the island from the *Scythe*. Each stroke was accompanied by the regular tick-clack of the sailor's joints as he worked the oars. If he was anything to go by, the crew of the *Scythe* was going to be like something out of a horror film. David felt a terrible dread at what he would see. Only fear of the unseen frapgins stopped him leaping over the side to swim for it.

The boat bumped up against the black and gold sides of the mother ship.

'What you caught?' called a voice, rough like steel-capped boots walking over gravel.

'I'm not sure, Captain,' called back the sailor. 'You'd better see for yourself.'

A rope tumbled down into the boat. David looked up. He'd only ever climbed the ones at school but now he had to scale what looked like a mountain from down here. This was going to be majorly embarrassing. He began to haul himself hand over hand. Above he was sure he heard a snigger. He felt a flash of anger and redoubled his efforts, gritting his teeth. Pulling himself over the rail, he collapsed onto the deck. A pair of black leather boots stood on the weathered planks in front of him. He raised his face, taking in the scarlet breeches, purple coat, gold neckerchief, long brown plaited hair and battered grey hat of the man before him. Yellow teeth like tombstones could be glimpsed in the matted growth of beard; a gold hoop earring glinted. Reluctantly, David met the gaze of two bloodshot brown eyes.

'What d'ye think, Master Farthing? Has old Bonebag gone soft?' said the man whom David assumed was the captain.

He heard another snigger behind him and an angelic-faced boy of his own age with sleek reddish-blond hair stepped into view. He was dressed in smart white trousers, blue shirt, and embroidered waistcoat.

'Soft as butter, sir. I'd've left this one to be food for the frapgins,' he said with a snide grin at David.

Bonebag climbed over the side in time to hear the criticism.

'He claims he's your kinsman, Captain,' he said defensively. 'Said Captain Fisher marooned him because of the connection.'

Captain Jones strode over to where David was still sitting and took a handful of his hair to pull him to his feet. Holding up a lantern, he turned the boy round, looking at him from every angle.

'Well, I'll be damned. No wonder he didn't like the look of you. What's your name, boy?' he growled.

'David Jones,' David replied trying to hide the distaste he now felt for his previously unremarkable surname.

'So, Shark Fisher has been up to his old tricks, has he?' said Captain Jones with evident pleasure.

'W-what?'

'Marooned you—damned you to death—turned you into food for frapgins without so much as a backward look.'

'I suppose,' said David, looking down.

'I knew it—I knew he hadn't changed!' cried Captain Jones exultantly, bringing his great fists together with a noise like a thunderclap. 'He's playing a long game, is old Shark. Thinks to fool me by "nobly sewing the worlds together"! Codswallop: he's after the gold too, or my name ain't Tiberius Jones. Marooning the boy shows that he's no better than he ever was—he's not changed one iota.'

The captain turned back to David with a frown.

'You claim to be my kinsman, eh?' he asked.

'Not claim, sir,' David said hurriedly. 'It was Captain Fisher that said it, not me. He said I looked like you did at my age.'

Captain Jones scratched his chin with his blackened fingernails and chuckled.

'That you do, sonny. Lucky you, eh? But it's been three hundred years since I was living on Earth; you must be a very distant relative.'

'Yes, sir. I'd never heard of you until I came here.'

This confession didn't please Jones. He picked David up by the front of his pyjamas and shook him. David had the belated realization that he was dealing with a psychopath when it came to the subject of Jones's own reputation.

'My own family forgotten me, have they? Not one of my sons dared mention me, eh?'

'I . . . er . . . I think my grandad might know; he's mentioned something, now I come to think of it. He might've been waiting until I was older to tell me,' David improvised. 'Until I was old enough to understand.'

'Hmmm.' Jones put David down and patted him hard on the back. 'Not bad manoeuvring, boy, for a young 'un.'

A grey parrot sailed out of the darkness and settled on Jones's shoulder. David thought for one wild moment that it was Jemima—that the *Golden Needle* must be near—but then he noticed that the bird had only one eye.

'What say you, Milli?' asked the captain, scratching the parrot's head. David was getting used to the captains on the Seas In-between consulting their pets.

The parrot squawked.

'Handsome fella, ain't he?' laughed the captain—and David was sure he meant the opposite. 'Well, take him below, Master Farthing, and see he is togged out in gear more suitable than those rags of cotton. Can't have him disgracing the name of Jones, can we?'

The captain turned his back and strode off down the deck, whistling merrily under his breath. The arrival of David, giving him evidence that his enemy was still a bloodthirsty pirate at heart, seemed to have tickled Captain Jones's humour.

'Make all sail!' he cried out to the crew. 'The *Golden Needle* can't be far ahead. She's sewed her last stitch, me hearties!'

The crew gave a cheer and above David, from the mended yardarm, a yellow canvas sail unfolded like a curtain coming down in the theatre.

'Hey you, toe-rag,' snarled Master Farthing once the captain was out of earshot. 'You'd better come with me.'

Disliking the boy more with every moment, David followed him to the hatch leading below decks. Farthing slid down the ladder without touching the rungs; David descended more cautiously.

'From my world, are you?' snapped Farthing as he ducked past the hammocks slung between the decks. A huge creature with hooves and a mane snored loudly as his bed swayed to and fro.

'I suppose so,' David said sullenly. He didn't trust this sly boy, even if he did look so innocent.

'Can't say I think much of your century,' said Farthing as he unlocked a heavy padlock on a steel-hinged door. 'Too law-abiding—too many of those mechanical eyes watching. How can an honest thief hope to make a living? It wasn't like that in my time.' He hauled open the door to reveal a storage compartment.

David was just about to leap to the defence of his own era when the sight before him choked off the words in his throat. The room was piled high with treasure. Bales of golden thread lay neatly stacked as if Rumpelstiltskin had been spinning straw for a year. He saw other treasures everywhere he looked: piles of rubies the size of duck's eggs in one casket; ropes of diamonds as plentiful as raindrops hanging over hooks in the wall; scores of silver goblets stacked haphazardly in a basket; a barrel of mixed gems like some bizarre lucky dip where every fistful would be worth a king's ransom.

'Beautiful, isn't it?' said Farthing, for the first time looking as if he had been sincerely moved by something. He picked up a nugget of gold and kissed it. 'It's taken years, but we've almost got enough now.'

'Enough for what?' David asked.

'To spend, of course, you oaf.' Farthing threw the nugget aside and poked David in the ribs with the key to make his point. 'We haven't spent all these years bobbing about on these damned seas for nothing. When the captain gives the signal, we're splitting the loot and each going our separate ways. I thought I'd be able to live quite well in our world on this—buy myself a little place—Bermuda perhaps—and live like a king.'

'But what if you can't get back? What if you cut one thread too many and Earth drifts out of reach?' asked David, wondering at the self-assurance of a boy thinking he could buy himself a whole country.

Farthing shot David a suspicious look. 'Been listening to the old wives' tales of Shark, have you, Davy boy? Got you steamed up with his worriting and fretting, has he? He's been saying for years that the worlds will drift apart if we carry on salvaging his thread, but I see no proof.'

'What about Tintel?' David ventured gingerly, knowing this was dangerous ground for a spy like him to tread if he wanted to keep on the right side of this crew.

Farthing picked up a handful of precious stones and let them fall back into their casket.

'Tintel? Who cares about little old Tintel? There was nothing but ice trees and snow flowers there—no earthly use to anyone.'

David might have said that he knew someone who cared but he held his tongue.

'Anyway, even if Earth does begin to drift off, as long as I'm home first, I won't care. Surely, it'll be a few years before it reaches the Inferno Rim—that should see me out. I've already had far more than my three score years and ten in any case, though it may not look it to you.' He touched his smooth cheek reflectively, evidently proud of his appearance of eternal youth.

David fumed as he heard this unnatural old-young boy speak so carelessly of the future of others. It was a struggle to maintain his silence.

'So, Davy Jones, let's see what we've got in the locker.' Farthing cackled as if he had just cracked a very witty joke while he bent over a chest full of clothes. David looked blank. 'Davy Jones's locker—the grave of drowned seamen—get it?'

'Hah!' David managed a strained laugh. 'Very funny.'

Farthing started throwing out miscellaneous items of apparel—a silk shawl, a striped cloth, a pair of boots.

'What about this?' he said nastily, holding up a girl's frilly dress. 'No? I thought it'd suit you.'

'No,' said David, unable to resist the taunt, 'you're the one with the looks for that.' He bit his tongue, realizing he wasn't doing a very good job of worming his way into the crew if he took to insulting them.

But Farthing laughed, appreciating a show of spirit from the new boy. He only respected those who could stand up for themselves. David appeared to have passed some kind of test for Farthing next pulled out a white linen shirt, blue breeches, and blue silk waistcoat.

'Try these for size, Davy boy,' he said throwing them at him.

David took off his battered pyjama top and pulled on the shirt and waistcoat. It was good to feel warm again after a night of shivering. The breeches were a little too big but he was able to keep them up with the thick black leather belt Farthing dug out for him. Wondering what sort of figure he now cut in his new clothes, he scrutinized himself in the mirror-like surface of a polished silver plate.

'I look like something from a pantomime,' he muttered.

'And the finishing touch!' Farthing picked up a plumed black hat and stuffed it on David's head. His face loomed in to the reflection alongside David's, his smile mocking. 'Just like the captain.'

David had seen that look on other boys before, usually on the first day at school just as they played some trick to get the newcomer into trouble with the teachers. He pulled the hat off and chose one with a smaller brim.

'I don't think I'll go into competition with Captain Jones, thanks.'

'Aw, spoilsport!'

Farthing stooped to return the rejected clothes to the chest. When David thought he was unobserved, he slid the lock of hair from his pyjama to his waistcoat pocket. But he had underestimated the boy's eye for treasure.

'What's that?' asked Farthing sharply.

David thought quickly. He didn't want to give the game away by revealing that he had friends still on board the *Golden Needle*.

'My own little treasure,' he said, holding out the lock of hair for his inspection. 'You like gold—well, I like silver. I nicked it off the cabin girl on the *Golden Needle* while she was sleeping.'

Farthing chuckled appreciatively.

'What! Off that wisp of a creature! Well, that's the first real sign you've showed, Davy boy, that you might have the captain's blood running in your veins. Come, I'll show you where you can sling your hammock. You get a few hours kip and then you'll be awake to see yourself revenged upon the *Needle*.'

Farthing expertly frisked David's pockets to check he hadn't stolen any valuables then led him out of the storeroom, locking the door carefully behind him. David noticed that Farthing had many such keys hanging on a chain at his waist. It seemed that he was far more than cabin boy on this ship.

Farthing spotted David's expression of keen interest. He swung round, bunched the keys in his fist and shoved them in David's face, jangling them loudly.

'Is this what you looking at?' Farthing asked.

David stared back, alarmed by the sudden change in mood.

'Well, don't.' Farthing slapped the keys painfully on David's cheek. 'You'd better learn one thing fast. You keep your nose out of other people's business and you'll keep your nose on your face. I'll happily cut it off if I find you prying into stuff that's no concern of yours. Don't make the mistake of underestimating me!'

Bonebag crept up behind the two boys and gave a wheezy laugh. 'Aye, Master Farthing, remember old Gil? He lost his snout to you for trying to count the loot, didn't he?'

Farthing gave a cruel smile. 'I remember it with great pleasure—I also remember he no longer looked quite so handsome without it, so you keep that in mind, Master Jones.'

David didn't know what to say. If they were likely to cut off his nose for merely looking interested in what was going on around the ship, what would they do when they found out that he was here as a spy?

'Come, I'll show you where you can hang your hammock. I know: I'll give you Gil's old berth. He doesn't need it any more, does he, Bonebag?' Farthing gave the skeletal man a grin.

'That he doesn't, Master, thanks to you.'

'Follow me,' Farthing called over his shoulder to where David was still standing, frozen to the spot, 'that's if you don't want to follow Gil over the side.'

Billeted in the dead sailor's berth, David lay in his hammock staring at the planks above him. Though exhausted, he could not sleep as the reality of what he had volunteered to do finally struck home. The pirates on board this ship were nothing like the gruff but friendly crew of the *Golden Needle*. Farthing in particular was the worst bully he'd ever met, worse even than Ricko and his gang. He positively relished his own cruelty and pushed it to extremes unchecked. If Farthing had been in David's class, the school counsellor would have had a field day with him if he had been sent to her office. The guy clearly had had a couple of centuries to work up a whole series of mental issues—behavioural disorder Premier League material.

David had yet to work out what the captain was really like. Fierce, yes; commanding, that too; but there was also a self-mocking sense of humour.

But he's bitter, thought David. *He wants his own back on Captain Fisher. So I guess I was only allowed aboard to spite his old friend.* David doubted that Jones would otherwise risk so much as a fingernail

93

to save a stranded sailor. Not like Fisher going among the snow bears to rescue Shushula.

David chewed his bottom lip. He'd done the right thing, hadn't he, volunteering for this mission? Fisher and the others had told him the truth about the golden threads? He wasn't the biggest mug in the history of the Seas In-between, was he?

He turned over, feeling the hammock sway and creak with the motion of the ship. But what was the truth? After all, did any of this exist?

Don't forget the pain and the fear in the fight and with the frapgins, a second voice chimed into his internal debate, *they were genuine enough. You have no choice but to act as if it was all real.*

That was true. He didn't want to find out what it felt like to be caught out as a spy on the *Scythe* even in a dream.

The telltale jangling of keys approached his hammock. Farthing was on the prowl again. David closed his eyes and pretended to sleep.

'Master Farthing?' It was Bonebag. He had been waiting respectfully in the gangway for the boy to approach. David wondered at this—a creature such as the skeletal man waiting on the pleasure of a little boy?

'Yes, First Mate?' said Farthing, businesslike as he checked all doors were secure.

94

'We're running low on stores, Master. If we don't restock now, we won't have enough to catch the *Golden Needle* when she's next sighted.'

David strained his ears to make out their low voices. They were talking about the secret of the *Scythe*'s speed, he was sure of it.

Farthing tutted irritably. 'But what of that last load we took on from Earth?'

'All gone, Master. We seem to be using more than we did before. Perhaps something's wrong with it?'

'Well then, I'll take a look. But tell the captain we'll have to call in at a port. I suggest Carl—it's nearest to our current position.'

'Aye, aye, Master. You know best.'

'As always, Mister Bonebag, as always.'

CHAPTER SEVEN
Punishment

W hen David woke from his first proper sleep for days, he found that a list of duties had already been set out for him. Master Farthing evidently wanted to keep him busy at all times, either to show him who was boss or to wear him down so much that he had no time for snooping, David wasn't sure. He tried to behave so as not to attract attention, scrubbing the decks as instructed until his back ached and his hands bled from the rough treatment.

Look at me! he laughed sourly to himself. *My first cruise—all sun, sea, and sand.*

His silent scrub, scrub, scrub, up and down the decks gave him plenty of time to observe the crew. Jones ran a tight ship, pouncing on any slackness in his men with a ferocious temper. David saw him knock a man out cold for coiling a rope the wrong way; a second sailor was sent down to the brig with blood running from his mouth after answering impertinently. David had no difficulty in sticking to his boring tasks having witnessed what happened to those who disobeyed.

Jones had ordered a course which took the *Scythe* out of the starlit seas into the sun, heading for a port on Carl. The light revealed the sailors in their full awful glory. There were many men of Bonebag's type—from a dark world called Damm as David learnt from Master Farthing when the boy came over to check progress on deck cleaning. Farthing sat on a coil of rope, sipping from a hip flask as he watched David hard at work, throwing the odd remark in his direction. Farthing liked to show off his superior knowledge to David, as long as it did not concern anything he thought important. This way David learnt that the captain's parrot, the bird he had almost mistaken for Jemima, was in fact Jemima's only chick, full name Millipede.

'Can't abide talking birds,' commented Farthing. 'I'd like to wring her neck but the captain won't let me.'

The next most noteworthy character on the ship was the cook, known to the crew as Mother Reckland. She was a heavy-jowled woman from Tarnis, with particularly unattractive grey scaly skin. Her cooking was no better than Halist's, not least because she wept the whole time, leaving salty traces in everything she touched.

'What's up with the cook?' David asked Farthing as he rinsed his brush in a bucket of seawater. His skin smarted with the sting of salt in his cuts.

'Oh, her,' said Master Farthing dismissively as he bit into a juicy green apple, making sure that David could see every tasty mouthful being swallowed. 'They say Tarnisians are unimaginably beautiful in their youth—but it only lasts a few summers and they all become like Mother Reckland. She left it too late to come to the Seas In-between: already aged into that crone. Now all that's left of her to tempt anyone is her gold teeth.'

When David lined up for his serving of stew, he noticed that she did indeed have a very fine set of solid gold teeth.

'Like the cuisine?' mocked Farthing as David passed with his bowl. He was dining on cheese and bread that he had got hold of from the captain's table. 'I never touch it. It's worse than the stuff they used to serve at my old school.'

'Can't anybody cook on the Seas In-between?' David muttered grumpily as a foul aroma wafted from the stew. He sat at Farthing's feet and took a cautious mouthful, keeping it down with difficulty. Memories of school dinners haunted his offended taste buds. *Sorry, but even Turkey Twizzlers are better than this*, he thought, putting down his spoon. 'You know, I think this is as bad as the stuff Halist serves.'

'Halist? Oh, that slimy creature from Scaranga?' said Farthing with a shudder. 'I can't abide snakes. Didn't expect him to be up to much in the galley. No, the only place for a crewman to get a decent meal is upon the *Wanderer*, according to the captain.'

'The *Wanderer*?' David felt he was on relatively safe ground to show interest in another ship.

'A ship of female sailors—they rarely let a man on board. The captain was invited once and took quite a shine to the captain. She's from Tarnis and still a beauty: skin the colour of honey and eyes like emeralds. The captain gave her a dagger inlaid with the jewels in their honour. Remarkable really: the only time I've ever known him give anyone anything.'

'And the cook?' asked David feeling very hungry at the thought of decent rations.

'A woman from Earth, so she's bound to be better than these Scarangans and Tarnisians.

Name of Sally Ann Bowers. If you want a good meal, Davy, I say you should jump ship and join up with them—but you'd better put on that dress I offered you or you've no hope. They'd never take a man on board while at sea—it's against their captain's rules.'

Farthing had grown bored with talking to David so strolled back up the deck, keeping an eye on the doings of the other men. David looked down into his grey, watery stew and then at the other crew members forcing it down with a bitter curl to their lips. Two of them had given up and were lining up a pair of hooded cockerels. A ripple of excitement passed through the crew and they began to cluster around the birds.

'A fight! A fight!' called one Dammian excitedly. 'I'll bet three gold pieces on the black.'

'Four for the red!' cried another, slamming the coins down on the deck.

The betting began fast and furious, hands and hooves flying, money rattling down onto the timbers. Edging away from the crowd, David noticed that Farthing had stepped forward to act as bookmaker to the crew, collecting all the coins and marking down the bets in a little notebook. He seemed fully occupied with the task. Even Captain Jones strode over, knocking David out of the way, to take a closer look at the cockfight.

I don't want to spend a day longer than necessary on this ship so now's my chance to find out what makes the Scythe *so fast*, thought David. Whatever it was would probably be behind one of those locked doors. If he could just work out which one in time.

He slid down the ladder and tiptoed past the crewmen of the next watch, eerily peaceful as they snoozed in their hammocks.

It's a bit like being in the belly of a whale down here, David mused, mesmerized by the sailors swinging to and fro in time with the dip and rise of the ship, moving together like a single organism. With all those unwashed bodies, it smelt as bad as the contents of a whale's stomach too.

Though the *Scythe* had reached sunny waters on its journey to Carl, only dim light filtered through the hatches and open gun ports. David moved stealthily from bulkhead to bulkhead, peering into each section of the deck. He started at the bow, looking for more locked doors. He found one near a rack of cannon balls, ran his fingers over the rough wood but could find no spyhole or crack to see inside. He put his ear to the door but could hear nothing. A second, in the middle of the ship, looked to be the brig as it had a small barred window up high and a stout lock. He bypassed the treasure room without a second glance—it was not gold and jewels he was after.

Just as he slithered along the wall past the strongroom, a sailor in a nearby hammock threw out an arm, knocking David's hat from his head. David stood flat against the wall, heart pounding, expecting a rough hand on his collar and blows. The sailor gave a snore and turned over, still fast asleep. With a sigh of relief, David picked up his hat and continued his search. Creeping to the stern, he guessed that he must now be somewhere under the captain's cabin. He paused, listening. He could hear shouts and catcalls from the deck. The fight had got under way.

How long would a cockfight last? he wondered. Probably not long enough. He had better hurry.

His exploration ended, as he expected, with another locked door. David had a hunch he was near the secret. He peered through the keyhole: it was completely dark inside. A strange smell hit his nostrils. He sniffed. What was it? It smelt like that stew of Halist's, made from the oily fruit Shushula had called gartan. They didn't have a store of that in there, did they? If so, why keep the door locked? No one in their right mind would want to eat it.

David heard the footsteps behind him in time to duck under the nearest hammock. It sagged under the weight of its occupant.

'Where's he got to?' he heard Farthing snap.

'Can't see him, Master,' said Bonebag. 'I see in the dark as well as any frapgin but I can't spot the boy down here.'

'I don't trust him. Like I said to the captain, he's not told us everything. We should've thrown him over the side as I suggested this morning.'

So much for your hard work, thought David grimly. Whilst he had been patiently scrubbing the decks, Master Farthing had been plotting his murder and keeping him under a close watch. It must have amused him greatly to talk to a boy he had condemned.

'Nah, you can't get rid of him,' said Bonebag.

Farthing struck with the speed of an angry rattlesnake. There was a grunt. The Dammian appeared to have taken a blow to his ribs.

'You dare question my judgement?'

'Not me, Master Farthing,' cringed Bonebag. 'It's the captain. He won't hear of it.'

This reply angered Farthing. David could hear his keys jangling on his belt.

'The captain usually takes my advice. So why not now?'

'It's not for me to say, Master.'

'Rubbish, Bonebag. You know the captain better than most. You must have some idea why this boy interests him. I can't believe he'd get weak over some slight claim to kinship. Speak, man.'

'I think, Master,' Bonebag was choosing his words carefully, 'he likes to see you a bit riled. The harder you push to get Davy Jones over the side, the harder he'll cling on to him—until he gets bored, that is.'

'Until he gets bored,' echoed Farthing. 'Well, in that case, I'd better make sure he gets bored quickly. I'm already sick of the whelp. I haven't got all day to look for him. We'll give him the lash and a night in the brig when he turns up. The captain surely can't object to us disciplining the crew?'

'No, no,' agreed Bonebag. 'He'll probably find it amusing.'

The two returned to the deck. David stayed where he was until he was sure they had gone. He was trembling, his skin clammy. His fantasies about life on board a sailing ship had been hopelessly romantic, he realized that now; the gritty reality had turned out much more brutal and uncomfortable. He knew enough about discipline on board sailing ships to fear the punishment in store for him. But then, he also knew it would only get worse if he delayed. Crawling on hands and knees, he hauled himself up the ladder and slunk over to his neglected bucket and began to scrub as if he'd never stopped.

'Davy Jones!' He heard his name shrieked out by Bonebag with great relish.

He leapt to his feet. 'Aye, sir?'

'Where've you been, boy?' Bonebag grabbed him by the arm and pulled him into the centre of the deck. The other crewmen stopped what they were doing to watch. It didn't matter to them if the spectacle was of a cockfight or a beating—as long as it broke the tedium of a day at sea.

David looked down at the deck beneath his feet and noticed that it was covered in black and red feathers, sprinkled with blood.

'I was feeling seasick, sir,' he said.

Bonebag stared hard at the boy, noting that he did look a shade green—not like the other humans on board. The Dammian was not to know that it was the thought of the punishment that had turned David that colour.

'Well, boy, you should know that we have no time for seasickness on board the *Scythe*, have we, lads?'

'No, sir!' chorused the crew within earshot.

Captain Jones heard the disturbance and came to see what was afoot.

'What's the boy done?' he called down from his station on the poop deck. Farthing slid to his side.

'Neglected his duties, sir,' Bonebag said briskly. 'Says he's seasick.'

'Ha!' barked Captain Jones. 'Carry on then, First Mate. I've no doubt you'll make him sick of the sea if he don't behave as becomes a Jones.'

Bonebag drew out a wicked-looking whip from the folds of his black cape. It had nine cords at the end. There was an excited murmur amongst the crew. David paled.

'As it's your first offence, you'll just get a taster and a spell in the brig. That should teach you. Neglect your duties again and you'll hear this little beauty sing long and loud,' the First Mate announced.

'No, no, Mister Bonebag,' said Farthing, descending quickly to the main deck. 'I think you are being too soft on the boy. Spare the rod and spoil the child, that's what they teach on my world.'

'Not in my time they don't,' muttered David mutinously.

Farthing met David's eyes.

'I think I'll mete out the punishment myself on this one.' Farthing took the whip and stroked the cords. 'Tie him up.'

Two crewmen seized David and roped his wrists to the rigging. His shirt was yanked up over his head. Next, so quickly David had no time to prepare, the whip lashed down on his skin. He yelped, but then buried his face in his shirt to stop himself crying out.

'What? Only one?' protested one of the crew as Farthing folded up the whip.

'Oh, all right then,' Farthing said with a coy laugh, like an actor bowing to the audience's desire for an encore, 'if you insist.'

A second blow raked David's back.

'Sometimes, you know,' Farthing said conversationally to his spectators, 'I wish I'd stayed on Earth till I was a little bigger. I don't really have the muscles to do this justice.'

A third strike and David's resolve to remain quiet snapped. He let out a cry.

'At last, the message seems to be sinking in,' crowed Farthing.

By the sixth stroke, David was conscious of nothing but the pain. He no longer cared if he was sobbing aloud.

'Well, that should do it,' Farthing declared. 'Vorgat, take him below.'

David's arm was seized by rough hands and he was dragged down the hatchway. Vorgat, an old Tarnisian from the looks of his scaly fist, took him to the brig.

'Sometimes we give men a light,' Vorgat said cheerfully as he padlocked the door closed. 'But them weren't my orders so you won't mind staying here in the dark, will you?'

'I'm not afraid of the dark,' David said tersely, not wishing to give the Tarnisian the satisfaction of knowing that he was scared. Of course he was scared, but no way was he going to show it.

'Nighty night,' said Vorgat and clumped away, laughing.

David huddled in the corner of the brig on the rough bench. His back smarted from the blows: it felt as if fiery nails had scratched him. His shirt was stiff with blood. Alone in the dark, a succession of fierce emotions swept through him, one moment rage at Farthing, next fear for his own life, then despair that he would ever achieve what he had set out to do. What was he doing here? When would he get out? He seemed little nearer to solving the mystery than when he had first stepped on board. All he had to report was that the secret was something to do with gartan fruit, but how could gartan fruit make the ship sail as if it had wings? Everyone on Earth was depending on him and he was a failure. Fury at himself and at Farthing boiled over and he punched the wall, now having bruised knuckles to add to his tally of woes. He shook it in agony, cursing his stupidity.

I won't give up, he vowed, nursing his hand. *I can't let Farthing, Captain Jones and the rest win.*

Exhausted, David tried resting on his side, biting back a yelp as his shirt touched his wounds. He closed his eyes, thinking back over the past few days. He had been dragged to the Seas

In-between unwillingly, a boy calling his mother for help, a kid who ran from playground bullies. It wasn't a very attractive picture. He knew he had excuses but he certainly hadn't been a hero.

But I did something brave. I chose this mission. He dug into his pocket and pulled out Shushula's lock of hair. No one had said this was going to be easy, he reminded himself as he tied the lock to his wrist where it shone faintly, giving a silver tinge to the drab wooden walls.

I've got to help save the Earth from these pirates if it's the last thing I do, David told the darkness.

His words took him back to the beach last summer, how his father had announced that he had a task to do—a task more important than his family.

Had he been faced with a choice like mine? David wondered. Was that why he left?

And the beach was a place where water met land.

David sat up with a jolt, then swore as his sore back screamed with pain. Perhaps his father was here—somewhere on the Seas In-between? It made sense surely? The Seas In-between had their own rules, exerting a special call on some people. If David, why not David's father, both related to Captain Jones? How else could Simon Jones have managed to disappear so completely, not contacting his wife and son, not using his bank account, or claiming any of his belongings on Earth?

The notion that his father might be somewhere close by heartened David as nothing else could. He now had an added reason to keep going as there was the possibility he might find his father again. He had been given a chance to make a difference, to help save the worlds—and perhaps even his own family.

Whoa! One step at a time, he told himself, even smiling slightly at his own over-eagerness. He was not there yet. First he had to discover the secret of the *Scythe*.

CHAPTER EIGHT
Raid on Carl

S tuck in the brig, David missed the arrival at Carl. The first he knew of it was the door to his cell being opened and Farthing shouting at him to hurry up on deck. David tried to obey, but hours of sitting made his limbs sluggish and the strokes of the lash still stung.

'Come on, you scurvy dog!' cursed Farthing. 'I need a porter—and I've picked you, so hurry up if you don't want another taste of the whip.'

Stumbling onto the deck, David found the crew organized into raiding parties. Some carried cruel-edged curved axes; others had empty baskets strapped to their backs. Farthing thrust a wicker basket into his arms.

'Don't tell me, stink-breath, you've forgotten how to fag for your superiors in your day?' Farthing jeered as David fumbled to put it on his sore back. 'Lord, Earth has gone to the dogs.'

David had had enough. 'Oh, just shut up, will you! I don't care what you think about my world.'

'I'll say what I like about your puny century. If I wasn't in a hurry, I'd beat you again for speaking to me like that. Get over the side.'

David struggled with the temptation to continue the argument. He knew he'd probably get the worst of it but he was fed up with being treated like dirt. Farthing, however, decided the matter by striding off to marshal the crew in line before David could respond. Swallowing his insult, he joined the end of the queue for the gangplank.

David followed Vorgat as he balanced his way down the plank. Pausing for a moment to shift his burden into a more comfortable position he gazed upon his first alien world. It hovered in the air just out of focus, like a landscape seen through mist. Each step he took down the plank, brought it into sharper definition. The skies were deep blue but he could still see the stars. The *Scythe* had moored in the deep waters of a river running through a forest. Tall straight tree trunks rose like cathedral pillars in all directions, supporting a rustling green canopy of large-leafed branches. The air smelt pungent as the rotting leaf mould released its heavy scent into the warm atmosphere. Flies buzzed around him, bright gold-winged creatures with black beady eyes.

Carl is a tree world, David realized, wiping a trickle of sweat from his forehead. A rainforest. No wonder Art was closer to a monkey than a human. The Carlians probably thought of the treetops as their roads. It would certainly be much quicker to swing through the leaves up there than fight with the thick undergrowth beneath as he had to do.

The line of sailors marched off into the forest. David followed, wondering what a gartan tree would look like. He inspected overhanging branches for the dark green fruit but saw nothing remotely like it. Despite his precarious position on the *Scythe*, he couldn't help but be excited by his first taste of exploration. Every step revealed something new and wonderful. They passed under the tallest tree he had ever seen; thick aerial roots dangled from its canopy and planted themselves in the ground. A rope bridge carried them over a slowly coiling river, waters turquoise. Huge lily pads floated on the oily surface, home to gold-skinned toads that looked venomous to the touch. The earth steamed as the day warmed up. Everything was damp. David's clothes clung uncomfortably.

Suddenly, there was a cry up ahead and the sailors began to run forward in great excitement, shouting and swinging their axes. They must have found the fruit. David speeded up too, noticing the first tree-houses overhead before entering a clearing containing wooden huts and market stalls. Only then did he see what the pirates were doing.

'The ghosts! The ghosts!' A Carlian very like Art swung by in the lowest branches, sounding the warning, a small baby clinging to the fur of her back. She seemed to look right through David, as if unable to see him, but she could obviously sense the presence of the raiders by the noise and disturbance they created. As if to make the point, an axe arced through the air to land quivering in the branch she had just left. Tables overturned and a hut burst into flame.

She ran terrified from the invisible enemy. David urged her silently on to safety as, fleet-footed, she changed course to evade the missiles.

'Don't!' David grabbed at Vorgat as he set off in pursuit of the Carlian mother, an ugly look on his face.

Vorgat pushed David aside but did not pause in his hunt. The only reply David received was a bruising thump in the back. Captain Jones stood behind, fist raised, glowering at him.

'Shut it, you maggot! This is how we do things on my ship. If you don't like it, too bad.'

David turned to look in horror at the mayhem the pirates were causing in the Carlian village. Tree houses were aflame. Men and women scattered in all directions. A small child, separated from its parents, wandered amongst the sailors, crying, not understanding the buffets and kicks it could feel but not see. David didn't care what the pirates would think of him: he had to do something. Ducking round Captain Jones, he dashed forward, picked up the child, and ran with it to the edge of the forest where a group of Carlians had just bounded into the trees. David gave the child a shove in the back to make it flee for cover, but then a hairy arm shot out of the nearest bush, knocked David flying, seized the youngster and pulled it into the undergrowth.

The Carlians were now fighting back. An arrow whistled through the air and buried itself in the basket on Vorgat's back. Others followed. Unable to see their marks, the Carlians were shooting near any disturbance in hopes of making a lucky hit. They missed the opportunity to take easy shots at Bonebag, who stood in the middle of the village clearing, calmly inspecting a stack of jars, but their aim suddenly got more accurate when the First Mate put his basket down. David realized that the things the pirates carried were invisible until separated from their owner. Keeping low, David crawled away from the bushes just in time to hear two arrows land where he had just been lying.

I suppose it's no good trying to tell you I'm on your side? he wondered bitterly. An arrow landed near his hand. *No, I thought not.*

Other villagers had scaled the trees and began to rain rocks and heavy fruits down on the raiders. Vorgat received a direct hit on his head and was knocked out cold. Two shipmates scooped him up under the arms and dragged him out of sight. Marking where the missile came from, Bonebag lobbed a round-bottomed jar into a burning treehouse. There was an explosion and a Carlian fell from the tree, landing with a sickening thud.

David was about to run to the Carlian's aid when something tripped him up. He tumbled and lay flat on his back, his head spinning, until kicked to his feet.

'You're not here to lie down, dog boy,' hissed Farthing, folding up the whip that had made David stumble. 'You're here to carry these.'

'But the man—'

'He's no concern of yours. Pick this up or I'll kill you.'

David met Farthing's eyes and saw that he was quite serious in his threat. He shouldered his basket as Farthing loaded jar after jar into it. Farthing seemed unconcerned by the arrows that fell about them. David's knees buckled under the weight. The straps cut into his whip-scarred back.

'Retreat! Back to the ship! Back to the ship!' roared Captain Jones, giving a last kick to a table laden with pottery. It fell to the floor with a crash.

The pirates, most now carrying heavy loads of the same kind of jar as David, began to jog back down the track to their ship. David toyed for a moment with the idea of slipping away into the trees rather than returning to the *Scythe*, but what would he do on a world where he was invisible to its people? If he stayed here, it was unlikely he'd ever rejoin the *Golden Needle* or get home. He would be breaking his promise that he would try and find out what was giving the *Scythe* her edge. Reluctantly, he trailed after the sailors with only Captain Jones behind him, encouraging him to go faster with frequent kicks and prods with his sword.

The ship came in sight and the sailors slackened their pace, thinking they were safe. But they had underestimated the Carlians. Two of them bounded from the trees just as the pirates arrived at the rope bridge. The Carlians used their knuckles to swing themselves forward, both carrying machetes in their teeth. David guessed what they were going to do—it was what he would've done in their place. He accelerated, reaching the bridge on the heels of Farthing. Then things happened very quickly. The bridge lurched as Jones jumped on to the planks behind him. David felt the rope give way on one side—saw Farthing throw himself clear on to the bank. Then the bridge twisted and tipped him and the captain into the river.

David sank like a lead weight, pulled down by his load. He slipped his arms free of the basket and kicked for the surface. When he reached air, he took a great gulp before the river current spun him into a rock. The river was deep, the undertow strong, and he had already been swept far from the bridge. He could see the pirates were running down the bank, trying to keep up with him. No, not with him, he realized, as he hooked his arm around a root trailing in the water. He could drown as far as they were concerned. They must be after Jones.

David glanced around him. There! He glimpsed the captain as he resurfaced a few metres away, arms flailing, mouth gasping, then he disappeared again.

'Stupid pirate can't swim,' David muttered, feeling a mad desire to laugh. After a brief hesitation, he dived into the water and swam down until he grabbed a fistful of matted hair. Jones was a dead weight, heavy with sodden clothes and weapons. David was running out of air. Releasing his grip, he surfaced, took a breath, then dived again. This time, he pulled the captain up, finding strength he did not know he possessed. Towing his burden to the bank, David first heaved himself on to the mud and then wedged the captain on a rock so his head was out of the water. He could do no more but keep him from being swept further downstream.

Minutes later, a pirate crashed through the undergrowth near him.

'I've found the captain!' Farthing yelled. He took off the scarlet sash he was wearing and tied it under the big man's armpits, anchoring him more firmly.

'As for you,' he hissed to David as he lay helplessly gasping on the mud, 'let me give you a hand.'

With a kick from his boot, Farthing knocked David back into the river. Before he knew it, David was snatched under by the current. This time the river did not want to give him up. He spun like a twig on a mill race, unable to slow his progress. He lost the skin of his knuckles on a rock as he tried to grab it. Stunned by the next collision with stone, he took a gulp of water and choked. The water was getting faster and faster. The noise thundered in his ears. He had a horrid premonition of what was coming. Struggling to catch sight of the river ahead, he glimpsed the water smooth itself like silk and disappear into nothingness. A waterfall.

I'm going to die! thought David in horror. *I'm going to die and Mum will never know what happened.* He thrashed against the current but it was hopeless. He screamed for help but no one heard him.

Then, quite suddenly, he went over—

And stopped, hanging in mid-air with the water crashing down just a few centimetres from his face. He couldn't understand why he was not falling. Was he already dead? Was this what death was like, the final moment prolonged for ever? Then why did the water keep on skimming over his feet and what was the sharp thing digging into his chest and under his arms? He risked a glance to his left and saw a branch snagged on a golden rope, tippling on the edge of the fall. It swung there for an instant, then was gone, swept away by water. He clung on tighter, realizing the same rope was all that was holding him up. The gold thread looped across the river at the very lip of the waterfall. He traced its course to his right and saw that it was secured to a bolt set in the rocks on the far side. And someone was standing by it, hand resting on the thread, watching him.

Mist from the waterfall hung in the air, obscuring David's vision. All he could make out was a shock of unkempt dark hair, ragged blue trousers, and bare chest. A shirt lay abandoned on a ledge nearby as if the man had put it aside to work. But he was no Carlian; he was definitely human. He held an axe in one hand.

'You there!' the man shouted, his voice feeble against the roar of the fall. 'Get clear! I've already half cut the thread. It'll snap any moment.'

David didn't need telling twice. He kicked up his dangling legs and began to edge, slothlike, to the bank on the opposite side of the river to the thread-cutter. He dropped to safety as soon as he could and rushed back to the bank at the brink of the fall.

'You can't cut the thread!' he yelled across the water. 'Don't you know the worlds will die if you do that?'

The man couldn't hear him; he merely waved as if he took David's reappearance as a sign that he had got clear. The axe fell again and the thread dropped limply into the water.

'You idiot pirate!' David screamed at the man. The human paused as he pulled his shirt back on and looked up sharply. Further words died in David's throat as he caught sight of the blue denim shirt. It couldn't be—could it? Not his father—his father wouldn't cut the threads.

'Dad?'

The man cupped his hand to his ear, straining to hear. The mist cleared for a second and they both saw each other for the briefest of glimpses— David, barely recognizable, wet and bleeding from recent cuts, his father, sunburnt and ragged.

'Dad!'

Abruptly, Simon Jones turned and disappeared back into the trees. David only realized why when Bonebag gripped the back of his neck.

'Survived then, eh, Davy Jones? I was coming to look for your body on the captain's orders. Not sure he'll be pleased to get you back.'

Bonebag's eye was caught by the glimpse of gold. He picked up the thread and began to reel it in.

'But this he will be pleased to find. Someone did our work for us.' He strained his eyes across the river. 'Did you see who it was?'

David shook his head, not trusting his voice.

'Some freebooter doubtless. Stupid, though, to cut the thread and let it drift. No profit in that.'

The boy was barely listening. He couldn't believe what he had just seen: his father was on the same side as the pirates, destroying the threads that sewed the worlds together. But why? Perhaps he didn't know what he was doing. But then why do it at all? Why not come home to his family?

Bonebag had furled as much thread as he could comfortably carry.

'I'll send some men to salvage the rest. We've got to get back.'

'No, I don't want to go,' said David. He had already decided that he must go in pursuit of his father. *How far would he have to go back up-river before he could cross?* he wondered.

'Hah, that's your game is it? Thinking of jumping ship? Well, not on my watch, you don't.'

Before David realized what Bonebag was doing, a pair of manacles were clipped on his wrists.

'No slipping away from me.' With a tug, the First Mate towed David behind him, rope coiled on his shoulder.

'But I can't!' protested David, gazing frantically across the river. Was that a glimpse of blue between the trees?

'Course you can, you whining pup. You have no choice.'

He dragged David back to the ship, whistling an eerie tune with a sound like wind blowing in empty bottles. He was evidently in the highest spirits for a Dammian.

'Here he is, Captain!' Bonebag declared on arrival at the *Scythe*.

Jones was sitting wrapped in blankets on the quarter deck drinking from a steaming mug, Farthing hovering at his elbow.

'Where did you find him?' the captain growled before sneezing violently.

'On the bank by the fall. Miracle he didn't go over.'

'Isn't it just,' Farthing sneered, his cold eyes glinting as they studied David's face.

'Got this as well, sir.' Bonebag threw the golden thread on the planks. 'Fair bit more where that came from.'

'With your permission, sir, shall I order a salvage team to collect the rest?' asked Farthing eagerly.

Jones shook his head.

'Nah, we'll sail down the coast and salvage it at sea. I'll not waste another moment on this flea-bitten stinkhole of a world.'

'And what shall I do with the boy?' Bonebag asked with an evil look at David. 'He tried to jump ship.'

'He dropped his load in the river too,' added Farthing, neglecting to mention it had been to save his own and the captain's lives.

'Shall I throw him in the brig? Put him to work on the pumps? String him up?' Bonebag's black tongue licked his lips at the thought.

'No, no,' said Jones, shaking off his blanket and standing up. 'Take those bracelets off him and get him some new clothes and send him to me. He is to dine at my table tonight.'

'What!' burst out Farthing.

'What, *sir*,' corrected Jones. 'You heard me. Bring him along when he's dry. I don't want him dripping on my Persian carpet.'

Under Bonebag's beady eye, David changed quickly and followed the First Mate to the captain's cabin. He was confused and frightened. It would have been easier to face a punishment; this offer of hospitality was so out of character for the captain and far more worrying. The last place David wanted to be right now was eating at the captain's table, particularly when his father was so close. If he was given the choice, he'd even give up his mission on the *Scythe* and just go to find his dad.

'I've got the boy,' Bonebag said in his rasping voice as he stopped outside the captain's door.

'Send him in,' replied Jones.

With a sharp dig in his back, David was sent stumbling into the cabin, almost colliding with the long table that filled the centre of the room. Its shining black wooden surface was covered with silver plates and crystal glasses. A pyramid of exotic fruits formed a magnificent centrepiece—pineapples, oranges, cherries, grapes. After days of hard biscuits and revolting stews, David felt his mouth water at the sight. A golden roast chicken roosted on a dish, ready to be carved; warm bread nestled under a cloth, waiting to be torn apart and smothered in fresh butter. A jug of sparkling water stood beside a bottle of rum—David's thirst clamoured to be satisfied.

Captain Jones was seated at the head of the table, carving knife in hand.

'Take a seat, lad,' he said, gesturing with the knife to the chair at his right hand. 'I expect you've got quite an appetite by now.'

David walked slowly over to the seat and sat down, his eyes watching the knife suspiciously.

Captain Jones began to carve the chicken, slicing away the drumstick to reveal white flesh beneath. He put a thick slice on David's plate.

'We don't stand on ceremony here, Davy boy. Tuck in.'

Not needing to be asked twice, David fell upon the food with a wolfish appetite, refusing nothing that was offered him, except the rum.

'No, I didn't have a taste for it at your age either,' chuckled Captain Jones, his grimy face cracking into a smile as he poured himself a glass.

'It was old Shark Fisher that introduced me to the fiery drop.'

David decided he'd better eat quickly before the captain turned on him again. He couldn't believe this friendly mood would last until pudding.

'Slow down, boy, or you'll choke to death,' Jones said affably, piling his own plate with food and eating each item by stabbing it with his knife.

David swallowed.

'But why——?' he began.

'Why are you here and not in the brig?' Jones finished for him. He slopped more rum into his glass.

David nodded slowly.

'Don't think I didn't notice your behaviour at the village. Not pretty to see a crewman so squeamish.' Jones crumbled up a crust of bread and threw a piece to Milli. She snapped it out of the air with practised ease.

'It's not that I was squeamish, sir. I just don't like . . . like people hurting each other.' David knew it sounded lame even as he said it.

'As I said: you're squeamish, but that can be beaten out of you. Old Shark Fisher soon knocked that nonsense out of me.'

David wasn't sure what to make of that revelation.

'So why am I here then?' he asked.

Jones gave a bark of laughter.

'Don't you think I know who fished me out of the river? Master Farthing wouldn't have got his little toe wet to save me. He'd've been quite pleased to see me sinking with all hands just so he could sit in the captain's chair. It was you who hauled me up from the bottom. I owe you my life.' He raised his glass in a toast.

'He pushed me back in, you know,' David added.

'Of course he did. He's a good pirate. I'd expect nothing less of him. He's almost as mean as Captain Fisher was in his day and that's saying something.'

'Was Fisher really so bad?' David couldn't keep the scepticism out of his question.

Jones cradled his glass, his eyes taking on a distant look as he lost himself in the past for a moment.

'No one knows Shark like me, lad—just you remember that now. That's why I know he's still the same ruthless cut-throat as he was then.' He picked up the knife and carved a second slab of meat for himself. 'Why, I could tell you stories of his deeds that would turn your hair white. There's many a town in the Indies that has been reduced to a cinder thanks to him. You thought we were rough with those Carlians today? Well, that's nothing to what he would have done. If he'd been there, he would have spitted the babies on pikes and slaughtered the rest.'

David put down his drumstick, finding his appetite had suddenly vanished. Could Jones be telling the truth? Was the man for whom he had risked the perils of marooning and for whom he was now spying the same pirate who had killed so many innocent people?

'I was as green as you when I first sailed with him. He forced me to face up to the ways of the world—dog eat dog, survival of the fittest, yes, it was a hard schooling under Reuben Fisher. I soon learned that money was the only thing that lasted, long after friendship, family, and even love have gone.' Jones gave a self-deprecating chuckle. 'You'd think to listen to me that I'll next be demanding violins to accompany my sob story. Am I going soft in my old age, Davy?'

'No, sir. I mean, I'm really interested in what you're telling me.' David hadn't been sure what answer to give but this reply seemed to satisfy Jones.

'But you haven't heard it all yet, because then Fisher up and told me that he'd seen the light, been offered a chance to pay for all he'd done wrong. Well, I knew it had to be a trick,' mused Jones, swilling his rum, admiring its colour in the lamp-light. 'A clever one, just as you'd expect from Shark Fisher. The old tune was wearing thin—we were getting old—we needed a new course. I told him I wanted to come along for the ride, and so I did. He took me with him when he sailed the *Golden Needle* from the Caribbean to the Seas In-between, but then the madness started.' He shook his head, still marvelling at his memories. 'He pretended not to care for the opportunities offered by the worlds around us. I told him that he was sailing through the richest pickings anyone could desire, but he bade me get lost. He was all for spending the gold we had gathered on Earth stitching the worlds together, or at least that's what he said. I knew it must be a plot to cut me out of my share, but I've taken it back since, and more besides.'

It seemed that Jones would not believe, no matter what evidence was laid before him, that his old friend could change.

'So how did you get the *Scythe*, sir?' David asked curiously, turning the subject to the matter that had brought him to this ship. He still knew far too little about her.

'Ah, the *Scythe*,' said Jones with a smile, taking a gulp of rum. 'Well, where do you think I got her, boy?' When David looked blank, Jones continued, 'From Earth, of course. Stole her from a strange place—a big harbour full of other outlandish looking vessels. Enlisted Farthing at the same time—he said it was a museum in his day. He was the one who insisted we made a few additions, scavenged from the ships that were there. He's a remarkably ingenious boy, as no doubt you've noticed.'

David said something non-committal.

'Like him, do you?' laughed Captain Jones. 'I thought not. He's got a way of making enemies, has that boy. You and him—now that reminds me of how I was with Fisher way back. Me the innocent; him the pirate-hearted devil after the captain's chair. Farthing's been with me for years now and I know him well. He sees himself as the next captain of the *Scythe* or my name's not Tiberius Jones. Just waiting for his opportunity to plunge the knife in my back, I've no illusions about that. He's made a good start if he wants to be the next captain: the crew live in mortal fear of him, which is half the battle. The other half is never to miss a thing. If I know him, he's probably listening at the door even as I speak, aren't you, Master Farthing?'

There was a scuffle outside and the sound of footsteps hurrying away.

Captain Jones laughed again. He turned to David and offered him a fistful of blood-red cherries.

'And that's where you come in,' he said, spitting a cherry stone at Milli who had been sleeping on her perch by the cabin window until so rudely awakened.

'Me?' replied David, wiping the juice from his fingers onto a linen napkin, staining it with crimson drops.

'Yes. Don't think I haven't been watching you since you came on board.'

David's heart began to race. Had Jones noticed his attempt to sound out the secret of the *Scythe*?

'You're brave. You're not afraid to disobey orders and take the consequences. And most importantly to an old man like me, you're loyal to your captain. All you need to do now is lose some of that innocence of yours and you'll make a fine pirate like I did. A couple of raids, a few kills, and you'll get a taste for the life, I've no doubt about that. After all, you've my blood in your veins, you tell me.'

David gulped, not meeting the captain's eye.

'You see, Davy, I realized when you dragged me out of that river that you're the closest thing I've got to a son.' Jones patted his shoulder. 'I never set much store by blood, but that made me wonder. Maybe blood will out even after all these centuries? And when I finally hang up my cutlass, I'll want to know I've left the *Scythe* in good hands.'

'I see, sir,' David ventured, his mind working fast as he imagined all the enemies on board he would make if he was promoted to captain's favourite. But it could also be very much to his advantage.

'Farthing doesn't have your personal reasons to hate Fisher,' continued Jones. 'He won't carry on the fight but will go off looking after his own interests. He's not fit to succeed me.' Jones bent forward conspiratorially. 'But you and me, we're in this together, aren't we? I want you beside me when we find the *Needle*, when I finally send Fisher down to the sharks he so loves. You'll like that won't you, lad?'

David knew what he had to say.

'Yes, sir,' he agreed.

'What's that?' said Captain Jones, cupping his hand around his ear mockingly.

'Aye, sir,' David rapped back.

'That's better,' said Jones, taking another swig from his glass. 'It's time we finished him—time the Joneses cleansed the Seas In-between of that liar. Death and damnation to him.' He raised his glass in a toast.

'Death and damnation,' David replied as was expected, but to whom he wished these things he did not say.

CHAPTER NINE

Fishing for Answers

After his dinner with the captain, there was a distinct improvement in David's position on board the *Scythe*. He was not ordered to return to deck scrubbing, but invited up to the poop deck to learn the basics of navigation under Bonebag's instruction. The Dammian was not a patient teacher, cursing David if he made the slightest mistake, but fortunately David proved to have a natural aptitude for the sextant and compass, as well as a good head for maps, and therefore Bonebag had little to complain about. He even paid the boy a reluctant compliment when David plotted their course accurately to bring them back to the starlit seas close to the last sighting of the *Golden Needle*.

'That was well done,' he muttered as he scrutinized the bearings David had worked out. 'I think not even Master Farthing learnt the art quicker.'

Farthing was within earshot, keeping close to David at all times as if he at least still suspected him of something. He scowled at the first mate's words and turned his back.

David acknowledged privately that Farthing was right to mark his footsteps so closely for, despite the captain's plans for him, he still intended to succeed in his mission and make his escape. He had to get back to the *Needle* and then beg passage to Carl before all trace of his father disappeared. But with the keen eyes of his enemy following him everywhere, he had no chance at any point during the next few days to carry out further investigations. Time was running out: they had come on the trail of the *Needle*—the unmistakable golden thread twinkling to the horizon—and were making good headway with a stiff breeze to fill the sails.

It was the middle of the day. David was leaning over the bow rail watching the turquoise water glinting below, pondering how he could gain access to the secret room. Down on the main deck, one of the crew was fishing. David watched him cast his line into the water and within a few minutes he had hooked himself a silver fish. The sight gave David the inspiration he had so far lacked. If he could not get into the room, perhaps he could catch his fish from outside? All he needed was a few minutes alone in the captain's cabin.

A heavy tread came to a stop beside him and he felt the captain's hand on his shoulder.

'Beautiful, ain't it, son? The sea sings when the wind is like this. There's nothing better in all the worlds than a fresh breeze and a promise of gold ahead.'

David stood up and turned to the captain. He was surprised to see the captain's hard face was softened by a smile as he gazed out at the waves. The sea moved him like nothing else could.

'It is indeed a fine day, sir,' David said respectfully.

Captain Jones steered David across the main deck and up to the wheel on the poop, gesturing the sailor on duty to stand aside.

'Here, lad, let's see how this lady responds to your touch. You can feel the whole ship humming when you have your hand on the wheel, alert to your every wish or whim.'

He lifted David's hand in his own powerful fist and wrapped it round one of the spokes on the edge of the wheel.

'Master Farthing, fetch our young navigator a box to stand on so he can see,' the captain shouted to the boy who was standing close by with a frown on his pretty face. The frown deepened to a scowl but Farthing did not dare refuse an order from the captain. He kicked a box resentfully over to David.

Standing on this platform, David grasped the wheel in two hands.

'Turn her five degrees to starboard,' said Captain Jones in his ear. 'Look, that sail there is slackening. We can catch the wind better on the course you've plotted for us.'

With Captain Jones beside him to help, David spun the wheel as directed, stopping it when the captain gave the nod. The rudder answered and David felt a slight shift in the ship's course. The wind bellied out the sails and the sounds of the ship change subtly, a deeper, more contented hum. He experienced a rush of pleasure, so keen that it took his breath away: he was steering a living, breathing creature that flew over the waters under the control of his hand.

'You felt that, didn't you?' the captain said. David shivered: he had, but he could also feel the sour breath of Captain Jones tickling his ear.

'You've got a real talent for the sea, Davy Jones,' continued the captain. 'You've more true feeling for the ship than Farthing there. He despises the old ways of wind and sail, preferring to put his faith in his own cleverness, don't you, Master Farthing?'

'If you say so, sir,' he said dutifully, though his eyes glittered with thoughts that did not bode well for his captain's longevity.

'I hear that Davy boy has outshone you in navigation too, Master Farthing,' the captain said loudly.

David wished he wouldn't rub it in like this: Farthing needed few excuses to hate David and this would only make his enmity worse.

'If you say so, sir,' repeated Farthing, anger pinching his milk-white brow.

'I do, young master, I do,' chuckled Captain Jones. 'With a little more study, I think he might be able to take over some of your duties with the charts. What say you, Davy?'

'As you wish, sir,' replied David. Farthing moved off in disgust. David seized his chance. 'Might I study the maps in your cabin, sir? I'd like to understand more about the Seas In-between.'

The captain thumped him on the back.

'Of course, lad. That's what I like to see: an enquiring mind. Get yourself below and see if you can work out where that blackguard is headed.'

'Thank you, sir.' David leapt down from the box and ran swiftly to the ladder to the main deck. Farthing was talking to Vorgat and did not see him go. Shutting and bolting the captain's cabin door behind him, David paused, breathing hard, looking round the room for what he needed. Milli was asleep in her cage. The table was cleared of the noon meal. A chart lay rolled up on a shelf on the wall next to a case of pistols. Sunlight shone in at the window, making the rich velvet drapes glow ruby red and the ties glisten gold. He grabbed the chart and unrolled it on the table, weighing it down with two candlesticks—proof of his earnest study if required. He then unlooped the curtain ties. The thick thread was familiar. Of course, Jones had amused himself by cutting off some of the thread that bound the worlds together to ornament his own cabin. David tied the two ends together. They made about five metres in length—it would have to do. Throwing open the window, he fastened one end to a candle bracket and cast out his line. It dangled below the windows of the cabins on the lower deck and past the undercut where the stern curved inwards. Knowing he had little time to do this risky thing, he climbed out of the window, caught the rope between his hands and his feet and shinned his way down.

Once outside, he found himself swinging in time with the rise and fall of the ship. Gingerly, he let himself down past the windows of the first mate's cabin. He glanced inside and almost cried out. Bonebag was sitting just the other side of the glass with his back to the window eating a late noon meal. Swiftly, David lowered himself hand over hand out of sight.

He reached the level of the undercut where the rope gave out. He hoped there would be just enough length to let him see what lay below, obscured by the jutting cabins. Letting himself dangle at full stretch, ignoring the protests from his arm muscles, he looked down at the water frothing in the wake of the ship. At first, all seemed perfectly normal. Then he glimpsed something sharp like a shark's fin but moving at the same speed as the ship.

'Arrrk! Arrrk!'

The squawk from Millie carried even to David hanging off the stern. She had woken up. No, she was protesting at being disturbed, he realized. As fast as he could, he scrambled back up the rope, past Bonebag, up to the captain's windows and heaved himself in. There was a thumping at the door.

'Open up! Open up! Or I'll call the captain!'

It was Farthing.

David pulled in the rope and stuffed it behind the curtain.

'Coming!' he shouted breathlessly. He stumbled over to the door and fumbled with the bolts.

'What kept you?' snapped Farthing irritably with a suspicious look around the cabin. The chart flapped in the breeze from the open window.

'I must've dozed off when I was looking at the chart,' said David. He had to get the boy out of here as quickly as possible. 'What do you want?'

'I've come for the captain's telescope,' said Farthing, pushing past David and into the room. 'We've spotted a sail.'

'You'd better hurry back then,' said David, grabbing the telescope from its stand by the window and thrusting it into Farthing's arms, 'or the captain'll get angry.'

'Know the captain better than me now, do you?' sneered Farthing, still looking around the cabin to see what had been disturbed. He marched over to the curtains and pulled them back to reveal the coil of golden thread. 'He don't take kindly to pilferers.' He held up one end of the rope and wagged it at David.

'I was just seeing how long it was,' said David, hoping to encourage Farthing along this less dangerous line of enquiry. He pulled out the silver coil of hair. 'I'd thought of twisting them together. What do you think?'

'Think?' laughed Farthing nastily. 'I think you are heading for trouble.'

'Oh well,' said David airily as if he didn't have a care in the world. 'In that case, perhaps I won't—not yet at any rate.' He took the rope out of Farthing's hands and replaced the two loops on the curtains.

'I'll tell the captain.'

'Tell him what? That you saw me admiring his curtains? I'm sure he'll be really interested—not,' David replied sarcastically.

'Master Farthing!' bellowed the captain overhead. 'Get back here with that glass at the double or I'll flog you until your lily-white skin is as red as a smoked herring!'

'You'd better run, Penny,' said David, settling himself back down with the chart.

Glaring at the boy seated in the captain's chair, Farthing quitted the cabin and slammed the door behind him.

Once he was gone, David sat back and gave an enormous sigh of relief. That had been close— too close. He got up and walked over to Milli. Opening the cage, he took the bird out and scratched her head. Plucking a choice grape from the bowl of fruit on a side table, he offered it to her with his thanks.

'I'm David Jones,' he said politely. 'I am in your debt, Milli.'

'Davy Jones!' she squawked. 'Davy Jones!'

He took that as sealing their friendship so brought her to perch on his shoulder as he returned to the chart. He wasn't really looking at the map. He was thinking through what he had seen. That shark fin—it wasn't a fin at all. He recognized a propeller blade when he saw one. The secret of the *Scythe* had been revealed. If he had put the clues together earlier, he realized he could have cracked it without making the dangerous journey on board. The black diesel cloud, the dying fish in the polluted wake, the throb of the engine—the signs had been there for him, a twenty-first century boy, to read but he had been confused by the sails, thinking that the *Scythe*, like the *Golden Needle*, had remained stuck in an era before the invention of the engine. No wonder the *Golden Needle* could no longer outrun her rival: she was a sprinter over a short distance with a fair wind; the *Scythe* could now beat her over long distance in any weather conditions, thanks to her technological advantage.

And the raid: it hadn't been gartan fruit the pirates were after—that smell had been oil. He'd already confused the gartans with petrol when he had first smelt the stew and that was what had set him off on the wrong track. The Carlians must have oil wells in their forest. They probably burnt the stuff themselves for light and heat. And now the *Scythe* had stolen enough fuel to make a final assault on the *Golden Needle*.

David had thought he would be elated having solved the puzzle, instead he felt tired and dispirited. A doubt had been gnawing away at him ever since he had heard about Captain Fisher's colourful past. How well did he know his shipmates on the *Needle*? Not well. He had spent so little time among them. So why was he risking his life for Fisher's crew? Did he believe all this stuff about the worlds drifting apart? Farthing hadn't seemed too alarmed by the prospect. He seemed to think there would be many years before the bad effects would be felt. Anyway, was it really his responsibility to sort it all out?

Milli gave a squawk as if she could read his thoughts. She nibbled his ear affectionately.

'What do you think, Milli?' David asked the bird. 'What should I do?'

The parrot flapped her wings and flew to her perch.

'You think I should take the risk and get back to the *Needle*?'

She bobbed her head. David wasn't sure if she really understood him but her answer seemed right. After all, since when had he taken Farthing's opinion as his guide? Had not Shushula given him a gift and Art saved his skin during the battle? Even Captain Fisher, though he may still have a little bit of bad in him, seemed to be largely good; the balance was entirely the other way round with Jones. It was worth the risk.

'Right,' said David, standing up abruptly. 'There are three things I must do then. One, I've got to get back to my ship; two, I've got to stop the *Scythe* from sinking her; and three, find my dad.' It sounded so simple when put like that but he knew it was probably impossible. Still, he had to try.

Milli whistled.

'I'll take you with me, of course,' said David to the parrot, 'if you want to come, that is.'

Milli hopped from foot to foot with excitement. David took that as a 'yes'.

'Let's do it then.'

CHAPTER TEN

Fire!

David rolled up the chart and took a deep breath before emerging from the cabin. He heard shouts from above and the sound of the decks being cleared for action. The pursuit was on. Milli flew to his shoulder and clutched his shirt tightly in her claws. The pressure of her feet was a comfort to him. He did not feel entirely friendless with her at his side. He mounted the steps leading to the poop deck.

'You're just in time, Davy,' roared Captain Jones, his face flushed with excitement. His blood was up and he was staring after the silhouette of the *Golden Needle* like a hungry man sitting down to a banquet. 'I was going to send for you if you had not come of your own accord. Look: something must be wrong with Fisher's ship! He's not running for the night but dancing around out there just begging for me to take a swipe at him.'

David looked out to sea and saw the multicoloured sails of the *Needle* billowing idly in the breeze. Captain Fisher was indeed not taking advantage of the stiff wind but wandering irresolutely, spinning his thread in great slack loops on the water. David's heart leapt: they were waiting for *him*.

'What do you think, Davy? Is it a trap?' Captain Jones passed him the telescope. David trained it on the distant ship and picked out small figures scurrying to and fro, preparing the ship for battle. He thought he caught a glimpse of silver in the crow's nest.

'He's seen us all right, sir,' said David, trying to keep his voice cool. 'He's preparing for a fight. Perhaps you damaged the ship more than you thought in the last battle? Perhaps he can't run?'

He knew full well that the *Golden Needle* was in good shape but thought it wise to encourage the idea that it might be lamed. It would lure Jones into close combat and give him a chance to jump ship.

Farthing came back, wiping his hands on an oily rag.

'I still say it's a trap, sir,' he said giving David a pointed look. 'I don't trust anyone from the *Golden Needle.*'

'You don't trust anyone at all,' shot back David.

The captain laughed, enjoying the bickering of his two protégés.

'Here, boys, stand beside me. You can have best seats in the house for the demise of Captain Fisher. Today's the day: no more shooting high for we're sending Fisher and his crew to the bottom of the ocean!'

'Your plan, sir?' asked Farthing.

'Shoot the bow of that ship to pieces, kill the crew, and take our chance that we can salvage the thread from the wreckage,' said Jones.

'A good plan, sir,' said Farthing respectfully.

David said nothing. His head was too busy with ideas for how to save his friends. He knew they were going to let the *Scythe* come in close to give him a chance. They were banking on Jones's greed for a prize meaning that he would spare the ship; they didn't know that Jones had finally determined on their destruction. The *Needle* was doomed unless David could even up the odds in the battle.

'Will you give him an opportunity to surrender?' asked David quietly, hoping Farthing would not hear the question.

'Surrender?' asked the captain in surprise. 'Whatever for?'

'Oh,' said David lightly, 'I thought it would be funny. Wouldn't it be a better revenge to see Fisher humble himself before you than to shoot him to smithereens?'

Farthing was about to sneer at the suggestion but he caught sight of the expression on the captain's face. Jones was scratching his chin and smiling.

'You're right, son. We might get the ship as a prize and still have a chance to throw Fisher to the sharks. That's what I call smart thinking. We'll signal for a parley. Run up the flags, Farthing.'

Farthing ran to do his captain's bidding. David had bought himself some time but wasn't sure what to do with it. He followed in the captain's footsteps as Jones paced the deck.

'What do you think he'll do, son?' asked Jones, unfolding his telescope and checking the signal Farthing had just run up the mast.

'He'll talk,' said David.

Farthing came back, keys jingling at his belt. Signal flags appeared on the mast of the *Needle*.

Jones read the response. 'You're right, Davy: he's agreed to a parley. We're to meet in the small boats. He doesn't want to bring his vessel in range of our guns—he's a canny man, all right,' crowed the captain. 'Prepare the launch, Bonebag.'

'Shall I get the manacles for him—in case he does surrender?' asked David, mustering as much show of malice as he could.

'What? You'd lead him away in chains?' laughed Jones.

'That man marooned me for the frapgins; I feel no love for him, I assure you,' David replied, not quite lying.

'Well, be quick about it. I want you both to come in the launch to witness the downfall of the great Shark Fisher. Give him the keys to the armoury, Farthing, then fetch my best hat.'

Farthing hesitated.

'Hurry up, boy,' growled the captain.

Reluctantly, Farthing chucked the keys to David. He caught them deftly and ran to the stepladder leading below decks. At the bottom of the ladder, he slunk into the shadows, heading for the stern. Fortunately, the crew were distracted by the onset of battle and were busy clearing for action. He reached the door and tried two keys before finding the right one. The lock was well oiled and clicked open smoothly. He slipped inside and shut the door. He knew what would happen if he was found here.

It was dark in the engine room. There was only one lantern swinging from a chain to light the great metal beast that crouched before him. He was standing looking down on it from a gallery that ran around three sides of the engine. To David's eyes, it looked cumbersome and old fashioned—an engine that his great-grandfathers might have used—but here on the Seas In-between it gave the *Scythe* her cutting edge. On a rack against the wall lay jars upon jars of oil. Next to them was a large spanner on top of a toolbox. David picked it up, ran to the edge of the gallery and dropped it down amongst the cogs and gears of the engine. That would have to do. He'd been here as long as he dared. Letting himself out, locking the door behind him again, he grabbed a set of manacles from the armoury and ran to rejoin the launch party on deck.

Milli fluttered from her station on the wheel and landed on his shoulder as David handed the keys back to Farthing.

'You took your time,' the boy growled.

'Ready, my lads?' asked Captain Jones. 'Let's go.'

With Bonebag rowing, the four of them set off across the short stretch of ocean between the two ships. David could see a small boat heading towards them. If only he could jump for it now! But there seemed little prospect of that. Captain Jones was sitting beside him and Bonebag had a case of loaded pistols at his feet. He would be peppered full of holes before he so much as touched the water.

'Here he comes, Davy boy,' Captain Jones said eagerly.

David twisted round in his seat to get a better look. Captain Fisher was calmly rowing himself. He could have been out for a holiday excursion, not a trip to meet his most deadly enemy.

'Ahoy! Captain Fisher!' called out Jones, waving his hat in the air.

Fisher shipped his oars and let the boat drift on its own momentum towards them.

'Tiberius, I see you've changed your ways. I never would have expected you to choose talking over fighting,' replied Fisher. His eyes slid to David but then passed on as if he had not noticed him.

'That was a suggestion of my newest recruit here,' boomed Jones, slapping David on the back. 'A most useful bit of jetsam.'

Fisher smiled, revealing two gold teeth that twinkled in the sunlight like fangs.

'You're welcome to him, Captain Jones. I've never met such a useless creature before—except one, that is, also of the name of Jones. Couldn't get rid of him quick enough.'

'Ah, he does have that effect on some people,' chuckled Jones. 'There are many on my ship that say the same, but I think he's turning out to be very promising, full of the most devious notions. After all, it was his idea to give you this chance to beg for mercy.'

A look of surprise flashed across Captain Fisher's face.

'He suggested it, did he?'

'Yes. So, how about it? Do you want me to smash your ship to pieces or will you surrender? I'll spare the crew, I promise.'

'But not me, I suppose?'

Captain Jones took a knife from his boot and began to clean his nails with it. 'Now, you know I'm an honest man, Reuben.'

Captain Fisher gave a hollow laugh.

'So I can't promise to resist the temptation to send you down to the boy's locker with a cannon ball strapped to your ankles.'

'Very funny, Tiberius. And you've dragged me all the way out here to tell me this? You must be getting addled in your old age. What made you think I would ever agree?'

Jones put down his knife and fixed his eyes on his rival.

'It's a test, Reuben. You know you've no chance against me. Today's the day I settle my score. If you really have changed, you'd want to spare your crew.'

David thought he saw doubt in Captain Fisher's eyes as he shook his head slightly.

'No? I thought as much but I had to be sure. When I found the boy marooned, I knew you'd not changed. You're still the same bloody-minded, red-handed pirate, Reuben, for all your moralizing. You'll still send your crew to the bottom of the sea just for the slight chance of saving your own neck.'

Captain Fisher sighed and picked up his oars.

'You still don't understand, do you, Tiberius? You don't believe that there are some things of more value than your own life—or even the lives of those who follow you.'

'The only value I know is gold—and how much it can buy me,' said Jones dismissively.

'Precisely. That's why you're still a pirate and I'm—' Fisher faltered.

'You're what?' sneered Jones.

'A man on the mend,' Fisher concluded with a shrug.

Jones seemed to hesitate for a moment, perhaps partially persuaded by the steady gaze of his old friend's clear eyes. But then he remembered the boy sitting beside him.

'Very good, Reuben. You'd've made a fine charlatan preacher, fleecing the unwary of their worldly goods. What of my kinsman, hey? What "man on the mend" would leave a lad to be food for the frapgins?'

Captain Fisher looked straight at David. 'A sensible man, Tiberius. The boy's as crooked as a bent sixpence. Anyone can see it just looking at him.'

David shuddered. The relentless stare of the captain of the *Golden Needle* half convinced David that he meant his words.

But he came for me, he reminded himself.

He came for what you know, a snide voice in his head replied.

'I tell you what, Jones,' said Fisher. 'Let's say I'll think about your offer. You send the boy over with me and he can bring the answer back.'

'Fired from the end of a cannon, I've no doubt, you heartless old rogue.'

'I'm not afraid to go, sir,' said David, a shade too eagerly, half rising in his seat.

'No, no, stay where you are, boy. If anyone goes, it'll be Farthing.'

The young master did not look too impressed by this idea.

'Ah, Jones, you rob me of the satisfaction of doing away with the lad by my own hand as I should've done and not left him to be rescued,' said Fisher with a fiendish grin. Was he covering for David or did he mean it? 'In that case, I'll give you my answer. There is no surrender. May the best man win.' He doffed his hat to Jones in farewell and picked up his trailing oars.

'In that case, you've wished me victory!' called back the captain of the *Scythe*. 'Row for the ship,' he muttered to Bonebag.

David kept silent, wondering how Jones would take the outcome of this interview.

'That was, indeed, very—' mused Captain Jones.

'Annoying?' prompted Farthing.

'No, boy, amusing.'

David felt relieved: at least he would get no blame for the delay.

'I enjoyed seeing Fisher squirming one last time.'

'Squirming, sir?' queried Farthing. 'I thought he seemed uncommonly sure of himself.'

'Believe me, he was squirming. He knows I've got him over the coals and will roast him slowly like a pig on a spit.'

The launch party clambered on board the *Scythe*. The instant Jones's feet hit deck, his mood changed. He barked out orders, sending the sailors scurrying in all directions.

'Shall I start the engine, sir?' asked Farthing officiously, his foot already on the stepladder.

'Nay, lad. We'll keep that until we can see the whites of their eyes. But stand ready for my order. Here, Davy, you come up to the bow with me. You can fire the first shot from the swivel guns. Aim for the plume of Fisher's hat. If you clip his wings, I'll double your rations for a year.'

Captain Jones led David through the gun crews to the front of the ship. Mother Reckland was passing between them, doling out gunpowder, weeping as she went.

'Dry your eyes, you old witch,' spat Vorgat as he primed his cannon. 'You'll ruin the powder with your snivelling.'

But Mother Reckland did not stop crying for anyone and continued to wind her way around the decks.

Captain Jones guided David to the swivel gun. Standing behind him as he had done at the wheel, he placed David's hands on the trigger.

'Now, get him in your sights,' he said, bending low beside the boy. 'Can you see him?'

'Aye, sir.' David could see the captain standing with his telescope on the stern, scanning the *Scythe*, looking for signs of a boy leaping overboard.

'He's almost within range. It's worth a shot,' whispered Jones eagerly.

David did not know what to do. Jones was so close he would notice if he misfired deliberately. Knowing that Fisher was watching did not make it any easier. Closing his eyes tight, David squeezed the trigger, praying his bullet would go awry.

Bang!

The recoil threw him back into Jones.

'Missed—but you got his windows!' announced Jones approvingly, setting him on his feet and patting his back.

David looked up to see Fisher training his telescope on him. *What would the captain of the* Needle *make of his attempt to murder him?* David wondered.

'We're close enough,' said Jones, with his arm on David's shoulder. 'Let's bring this lady to life and out-manoeuvre the old pirate. Gunners— stand by! The boy'll give the signal to fire. Farthing, get below!'

David knew he had only seconds to make his escape, but he had the captain's hand gripping his neck as he waited for the *Scythe* to swing alongside the *Needle*.

'That'll do, lad. Give the order.'

David had no choice. 'Fire!' he roared at the top of his voice.

At the very moment he gave this command, all hell was let loose. The guns on the starboard side rang out, answered by the port side guns on the *Needle*. Underneath this commotion, the engines of the *Scythe* stuttered into life. Cannonballs whistled overhead. One hit the iron prow just metres away with a clang, bending the spike like a broken nose. The report of the guns died away, leaving just the rumble of the engines.

The engines were running. Had his sabotage attempt failed?

Clunk, clunk, grrrr.

Horrid squeals of metal on metal suddenly rent the air. The *Scythe* juddered and jolted. Great gouts of black smoke belched at the stern from the struggling engines.

'What the blazes!' swore Captain Jones, tightening his hold on David's shoulder.

The *Scythe* slowed. The engines ground to a halt. She was dead in the water. Farthing erupted from below decks screaming, pointing madly towards the captain, his pale face black with oil.

'It was him, sir!' he yelled, his finger stabbing at David. 'He's done it somehow! The engines are ruined!'

As quick as an eel, David spun out from under the captain's arm and made a desperate dash for the side. But he was not quick enough. Jones hooked him by the back of his waistcoat and threw him to the floor.

'Is it true?' he roared.

David made a second scramble for the side but was knocked back again.

'Trying to flee are you?' howled Jones. 'Then it must be true!'

Jones raised his foot to stamp on David's head. David rolled over and over to get out of range of the black boot, tumbling down from the bow onto the main deck. He struggled to his knees, only to find himself in the middle of a ring of angry sailors.

He would have been torn limb from limb if the *Golden Needle* had not intervened. A second barrage from the guns smashed into the side of the ship, reminding the crew they still had a battle to fight. With no engines they were a sitting duck.

'Back to your guns!' bellowed Jones. He jumped to the main deck and picked David up by the hair. 'And someone put this traitorous brat in the brig. I'll deal with him later.'

Bonebag scuttled forward and pushed David below decks. He fell to the bottom of the ladder, winded and dazed. Bonebag leapt down after him and dragged the prisoner to the cell, shoving him inside with no ceremony. The door clanged shut.

David lay on the floor. It was now the second time he had been in the brig but this time he knew there would be no escape. When that door opened again, they would be taking him to his death. He curled up into a ball and wept.

CHAPTER ELEVEN
Walking the Plank

T he sounds of battle had died away. David heard the boom of the *Needle*'s guns getting fainter and fainter and he knew that Fisher and his crew had given up waiting for him. It made no sense for them to hang around in range of their enemy's guns once they realized they had the advantage of speed and manoeuvrability over the *Scythe*. Not unless they were going to sink her—and David doubted they'd do this while he was still on board. He half wished they would. Death in battle now seemed preferable to what was to come.

He raised himself from the floor and rubbed his eyes, determined to die bravely if nothing else. He waited.

A key turned in the lock and the door swung open. Bonebag stood outside holding a lantern. He had pulled his hood up so David could not see his face.

'Come!' he rasped.

Two other sailors stood behind him, both with swords. David got to his feet and walked out, trying to keep his back straight and his chin up. He had nothing to be ashamed of: he'd taken a gamble and failed, but at least he had stopped the *Golden Needle* being sent to the bottom of the sea.

When he got out on deck, he found the entire ship's company lined up in rows. Stars twinkled on his right; on his left, faint sunlight shone. They must have drifted into the waters edging the starlit sea. The ship had suffered considerable damage in the battle. David noticed that the foremast had gone completely, leaving only a stump. He was not surprised that the ranks of sailors all seethed with silent malice, blaming him for every scratch, every injury they had sustained.

Captain Jones was standing by the rail, dressed in scarlet and black. Farthing stood by his side, a look of satisfaction greased all over his face.

'Bring the prisoner forward,' barked the captain, looking at David with great distaste.

A sword was prodded into David's back and he stumbled forward.

'David Jones,' boomed out the captain, 'you are charged with mutiny and sabotage. The penalty for this is death. What say you: guilty or not guilty?'

David did not hesitate. 'Guilty.' There seemed little point stringing this out: he knew they were after his blood.

'I should've known better than to trust to blood,' muttered Jones, turning his back on the boy.

Out of the darkness came the whoosh of wings. Milli settled on David's shoulder and nibbled his ear. He scratched her head and gave her a quivering smile.

'No, Milli, you'd better not come with me this time. There's no return from where I'm going.'

'Too right, you dog!' scowled Jones, his moment of regret stamped out like a beetle beneath his boot. 'The penalty for mutiny is to walk the plank.' He shoved his face up to David. 'The sharks like the waters where the starlit seas meet the sun. We'll enjoy watching them strip your bones.'

David's knees almost gave way.

'Going to faint, are you, you girl,' jeered Farthing.

David shook his head, refusing to give them the pleasure of seeing him beg for mercy. He knew they would show him none.

'No, Penny. I was just thinking what a relief it will be to get away from you. You're welcome to him, kinsman,' David said, addressing himself to Jones, 'but I'd watch your back if I were you.'

'But it was you who betrayed me,' spat Jones. He beckoned to a drummer to stand forward. 'Begin.'

The drummer rapped out a remorseless beat, each blow like a kick in David's stomach. The sword at his back prodded him forward. David walked to the rail and stepped up onto the plank. It seemed very narrow as it stretched out into nothingness before him.

'Here, Milli, this is where you get off,' he said, brushing the bird from his shoulder.

Milli squawked, flapped her wings, and launched herself into the night, heading out to sea.

'Good riddance,' said Jones, watching his parrot fly away into the darkness. 'Another traitor if ever I saw one. Well, Davy Jones, any last requests before you walk?'

David shook his head. He bit his lip, not daring to look down.

'Then, off you go.'

Jones unsheathed his cutlass and jabbed him in the back. David took two steps forward and stopped. He couldn't do it; he couldn't make himself jump.

The crew jeered, baying for his blood.

'He's bottling out. We'll have to throw him in,' sneered Farthing.

That did it. David broke into a run and sprinted the length of the plank, taking a dive off the end. He plunged head-first into the cold water—his first ever high dive—and began to swim away from the ship. If the sharks were going to get him, he wanted it to be in private and not in full view of Farthing.

'Oi! Stay where we can see you suffer!' bawled Farthing at David's fast disappearing back.

'Shoot him someone!' commanded Jones. 'The blood will bring the sharks all the sooner.'

David heard several loud bangs behind him and the water near his head was pocked with bullets. He kicked harder, making for the darkness, which was now settling around him like a blanket.

'He's gone, sir,' Farthing whined. 'You should've spilled his blood before you sent him over the side.'

'Shut it, boy.' David heard a slap. 'Don't try to tell me how to do my job. He's a goner—that should be enough to satisfy even you. Haven't you got an engine to mend? Bonebag, set a course for nearest landfall.'

David trod water for a moment, listening to the sounds of the ship preparing to depart. Then, thinking of the sharks that could be nosing about beneath him even now, he struck out for the starlight, a lone figure in an endless sea as the *Scythe* set sail for the sun.

He swam as far as he could before exhaustion overcame him.

This is it, he thought, feeling strangely detached and calm as the sea rocked him. I'll float here as long as I can and then . . . and then nothing. He spread out, floating like a starfish, and closed his eyes.

'Aark!' A harsh croak woke him with a start. He took a mouthful of water and coughed.

'Milli!' he spluttered.

The parrot was circling overhead, starlight shining softly on her powder-grey wings.

'Find yourself an island—find something!' David gasped. 'You'll die if you stay with me.'

He stopped speaking. There, bobbing about in front of him, was a great shaft of timber, still trailing ropes and canvas: the foremast of the *Scythe*, lost in the last encounter.

'Milli! You're a wonder!' marvelled David, hauling himself up and astride the raft. He lodged himself against the yardarm. Now out of the water he was no longer content to let himself drift off to death. The instinct to survive beat strong in his veins, but he was shuddering with cold.

166

Milli spiralled down and pecked at the tatters of trailing canvas. David understood. He hauled on a line and landed a large scrap. It shed water as he held it up, but after he had wrapped its stiff material around his shoulders, he felt the benefit of its protection from the chilling night breeze.

'You're a good friend, Milli,' David said through chattering teeth. 'You've found me my raft, got me shelter. Any chance of finding me a lift?'

Milli launched herself off again and flew into the night.

'No, Milli!' shouted David to the departing bird. 'I was only joking. Stay, please!'

But she was gone. David cursed his light words for depriving him of the only friend he had in this desolate ocean. How would she ever find him again?

As the question flickered in his mind, he felt the answer burning in his pocket. Of course: Shushula's lock of hair—as good as a beacon to a sharp-eyed bird. He dug it out and tied it round his wrist, letting the end flutter in the breeze like a tiny flag. All he could do now was wait.

Time passed slowly and David sensed a change come over the sea. The gently undulating waves that embraced him earlier had turned angry and were chopping at the mast, slapping

167

and splashing David with cold spray. The wind was more insistent: Shushula's lock of hair whipped to and fro like a snake trying to escape a trap.

Great, thought David, a storm. That was all he needed.

'Aark! Aark!'

Milli was back, looking very pleased with herself.

'Where've you been?' asked David, scratching the downy feathers of her breast.

'Man overboard!' screeched the parrot suddenly. 'Man overboard!'

David put his fingers in his ears.

'Look, I know I'm overboard. There's no need to rub it in.'

'Man overboard! Man overboard!'

Milli seemed to have become quite demented. She wouldn't stop shrieking.

'Shut up, Milli!' shouted David, losing his temper. He could feel the fear that he had managed to suppress on the verge of taking over. The stupid bird was driving him into a panic. 'Shut up!'

'Ahoy!'

David's voice died in his throat. He thought he had heard something.

'Is there someone out there?' a faint voice called.

David turned round on his narrow perch to see a great bank of lights bearing silently down on him. It was a ship under sail—but not the *Needle* nor the *Scythe*. If Milli hadn't made so much noise, they would never have noticed him adrift on his tiny raft. But that didn't matter now: it was his way out of here.

'Yes!' screamed David at the top of his lungs. 'Here!'

Pales faces appeared at the bow, staring out into the night. David waved his silver distress flare on his wrist.

'There!' shouted a sailor. 'And look, that mad bird's with the castaway.'

'Throw a rope. Let's see what we've caught,' commanded a second voice.

A line snaked out of the darkness and fell across David's raft. He gripped it but was too cold and exhausted to contemplate climbing up the mountainous side of the ship that was now passing him by.

'Tie it around you,' called the first voice.

David fastened the rope around his waist and immediately felt a tug tumble him into the water. He didn't stay there long: soon he was being hauled up the wooden sides of this strange vessel whose planks seemed to glimmer ashy silver in the darkness. He fell onto the deck and lay there panting, sending up silent prayers of thanks for his rescue.

'Oh, starfish!' muttered someone close at hand. 'It's a boy. We'd better throw it back in before the captain finds out what we've done.'

David jerked to his feet and looked wildly round for something to cling on to. He wasn't going back over the side if he could help it. Milli squawked indignantly and pecked at the feet of the offending sailor—a tall, willowy female with skin the colour of the silver birch under the peeling bark.

'Please don't!' begged David. 'I'll die!'

The second sailor bustled into view: she was a buxom woman with rosy cheeks and a mass of white-blonde hair tied back in a bun.

'You're from Earth, aren't you, sonny?' she said huskily, her breath laced with gin. 'How did you get here?'

That seemed a very long story to tell just now, particularly when the willow woman was talking about chucking him overboard.

'Please, I'm so tired. Just take me to land and I'll promise I'll never bother you again.'

The Earth woman chuckled and pulled him to his feet, tucking him under her arm.

'Sally,' whispered the other, 'you know what she says about men.'

'Oh, he's no man, Mia. He's just a boy. I'll look after him. She needn't know just yet. Look, the poor lamb is freezing. Let me dose him up and we'll worry about the captain later.'

Mia shrugged and coiled up the rope.

'On your head be it,' she said grimly.

'I can remember the faces of too many young people that I've ruined; it would be good to add the eyes of someone I've saved,' said Sally, towing David with her. Milli flew to his shoulder, squawking her approval.

'Hush, birdie,' hissed Sally. 'If you wake her, I'll not be answerable for the boy's fate.'

Milli clicked her beak shut with a snap.

'And as for you lot,' Sally addressed her fellow sailors, 'keep this to yourselves or I'll put laxatives in your food for a month.'

With that threat, the sailors on duty, all females of many species, Carlians, Dammians, Tarnisians, returned with renewed interest to their tasks, pretending not to see David pass. Having crossed the length of the main deck, Sally opened a door and led him into the galley. An iron stove glowed in one corner, chimney vented to the stern so that cooking smells and smoke would not distract the crew. But David found himself distracted now: warm, wonderful scents filled the cabin. He remembered how hungry and thirsty he was and almost fainted. It was like a traveller in a desert suddenly being deluged in a cool shower of rain.

'Here, sonny, pull up a pew,' said Sally, pushing him to the table. 'I expect you could do with some victuals inside you.'

She ladled a rich brown stew from a pot on the stove into a bowl and pushed it towards him. Having good reason to fear the food on strange ships, David sniffed it doubtfully.

'Eat up, it won't kill you!' laughed Sally, pouring him a tankard of sparkling water.

He took a hesitant mouthful. His taste buds exploded with delight—it was delicious! Beef in gravy, he thought as he spooned it quickly into his mouth.

'Take it easy, sonny,' chuckled Sally as she fed Milli some peanuts. 'You're eating that as if there's no tomorrow.'

'I didn't think there would be for me,' mumbled David through a mouthful. He next gulped down the water and dried his mouth on the back of his hand.

'That's a rare trinket,' said Sally, eyeing the bracelet of hair curiously as she filled up his bowl a second time.

'I got it from Shushula, cabin girl—'

'On the *Golden Needle*,' finished Sally. 'Aye, I

know that little Ariel. A fine lass. So how did Fisher lose you overboard?'

'He didn't,' said David, breaking off a chunk of bread to soak up the gravy. 'That was Captain Jones. He made me walk the plank.'

'Well, well, well, I can see there's more to you than I first thought.' Sally began to clear away the cooking utensils she had used as the cabin began to pitch and roll in the approaching storm. 'What did you do to annoy old Tiberius? Now you mention it, you look just like he did at your age—the resemblance is uncanny. Are you related?'

'Many times removed,' David said quickly, wondering how Sally knew Captain Jones.

'I should've seen it at once but I'm getting forgetful after all these years. Tiberius was a rare dog in his youth. Had all my girls running after him.'

'Do you know Captain Fisher too?'

'Intimately, my dear. Lost my heart to him when I was not much older than you. No good it did me, I can tell you. He was rotten—rotten to the core, I'd've said, if these seeds of the new man hadn't managed to sprout out here. He's got further along the road to making amends than me; I'm not yet sure I'm ready for that journey. Maybe I'll start with you.'

She smiled at him, lines at the corners of her blue eyes crinkling. David smiled back. He felt he could trust her. He pushed his plate away, realizing he already knew where he was.

'This is the *Wanderer*, isn't it? I was told how good your cooking was.' He gave a small burp, which seemed to please Sally even more than the compliment.

'That's what I like to see: a good healthy appetite in a growing boy. Some of the crew are so picky, you wouldn't believe it! Yes, you're on the *Wanderer*—lucky to be here as you'll only find one other male on board. There's not even a cock to keep our hens amused. I'm Sally Ann Bowers, chief cook and bottle washer.'

'And your captain—I've heard about her too.'

'Stella Tor—the most beautiful captain on the Seas In-between, but she's got an ugly temper, so don't be taken in by her honey skin and flashing green eyes like so many are.'

'And what are you doing here?' asked David. 'Are you after the golden thread too? Are you pirates?'

Sally laughed. 'Not us: we're just wandering for the adventure of it. That's not to say we don't cut a thread now and again if we come across one. Not so much as to do too much damage but just enough to let Shark Fisher know we haven't forgiven him.'

'Forgiven him?' David had a bad feeling about this.

'He stole Stella's gold. Wined and dined her on his ship—though the food wasn't up to much I hear—and told her it was to save the worlds from drifting apart. He'd run out of his own gold so had to have hers. She didn't agree. They fought a duel. He won—and took the gold. She spent six months with her arms in a splint and has never forgiven him—though some would say he won it off her fair and square.'

'Ah, I see,' muttered David. This was going to complicate getting back to the *Needle* somewhat. 'And what does she think of Captain Jones?'

'Oh him,' said Sally dismissively, taking David's empty bowl from him. 'Thinks he's a bit of a bore. He chases after her, you see, flatters her when she gives him the chance.'

'Do you think . . . ' began David, 'do you think she'll hand me back to him?'

Sally paused, hand arrested in the act of drying the tankard with a bright cotton cloth. She frowned.

'She might just do that. From what you say, Jones would love a second chance to finish you off good and proper. It might just tickle her fancy to let him.'

Something stirred in the corner, making David jump. He was now so on edge that he expected the captain of the *Wanderer* to leap on him at any moment. Sally, however, did not look alarmed. She plucked some leaves from a lettuce hanging up in a net and threw them to the floor. An enormous old turtle shuffled forward and began to munch them dolefully.

'This is Michael, the other male I told you about,' Sally said, sitting down on the great polished shell of the beast and yawning. Michael sank a few centimetres lower but carried on eating with a resigned expression on his sad face. 'He's my emergency ration.'

'Emergency ration?'

'In case we run short. You know, turtle soup. He'll feed us all for weeks, won't you, you great lump.'

Michael raised his dark eyes to her with a solemn expression.

'Ach, you silly old beast,' laughed Sally, scratching him under the chin. 'As if I would!'

But David wasn't so sure. He thought the turtle right to be concerned.

'So, David Jones, what shall we do with you, eh?' mused Sally. She straightened out her apron over her scarlet skirt and folded her arms.

David shrugged.

Sally looked up at the swaying lantern thoughtfully.

'Well,' she said, 'I don't think you need worry for a few hours. This is going to be a mother and father of a storm if I know anything about the sea, which means her ladyship will have her hands too full to worry about rumours of a stowaway. I suggest you stay snug in here with Michael and wait for it to blow out. You look as though you could do with a good sleep. A new day often brings new counsel.'

Having swum as far as he was able and eaten as much as his stomach would hold, David felt more than ready for sleep. His eyes were already closing of their own accord. He muttered his agreement and slid down to wedge himself between Michael and the wall, the only way to stop himself from rolling from one end of the cabin to another like an empty bottle in this swell. Sally threw a knitted quilt over him, stowed the last of the loose items away and blew out the lantern. Then wrapping herself in a heavy oilskin cloak she made her way back out into the storm.

David was asleep even before the door clicked closed, dreaming that he was being rocked in a cradle by a big shark with gold teeth.

CHAPTER TWELVE
The Wanderer

David woke up to find himself eye to eye with the turtle. Michael was staring at him with steady curiosity that was unnerving. The ship gave another lurch. The pans hanging on hooks clanged like cracked bells. David sat up and stretched. He felt refreshed despite his strange dreams; he must have been asleep for some time. Clinging onto the dome of Michael's shell, he stumbled to his feet, but was immediately sent rolling over the top of the turtle to crash into the cabin door. The ship pitched the other way and he rolled back to Michael.

'Not a good idea to move,' he muttered, wedging himself back between the turtle and the wall. Looking round for Milli, he spotted her roosting on one of the pans, sleeping through the jangling and jolting like the seasoned sailor she was.

David had not been sitting there long when Sally burst back into the cabin, her cloak streaming water onto the floor as if she had been standing fully clothed in a shower. She banged the door behind her.

'The storm's lessening,' she said, shaking water from her sodden skirts. 'Time we cooked breakfast for the crew. They've worked hard all night with only hard tack but I think I can risk a fire now. You can lend a hand.'

David scrambled to his feet, finding it hard to believe that the tempest was really blowing itself out as the cabin gave another stomach-churning lurch.

'You can cook the bacon,' said Sally, taking a smoked ham off its hook in the ceiling and expertly slicing some thin rashers. David watched her roll with the movement of the ship as she wielded the cleaver onto a butcher's block. He staggered to stand by the stove and took down a heavy iron pan. A sudden thump as a wave caught them broadsides made him drop it on his foot. He swore.

Sally laughed. 'Now, now, young man, language!' She walked over to the stove and stirred the embers of the banked-down fire. 'Here, first build up a good blaze.'

She left David feeding coal into the grate as she began kneading some dough. Once he had a fire roaring, David threw six rashers into the pan. The sizzling smells made his mouth water again.

'How many shall I do?' he asked, eyeing one of the rashers hopefully.

'The whole ham,' said Sally. 'There are sixty hungry mouths to feed.'

After cooking a stack of rashers, David moved on to scrambling eggs. He dropped three during one deep roll in the waves but Sally just laughed.

'Don't worry, Michael will clear them up,' she said cheerfully, beckoning the turtle forward.

David grinned. How different from his recent tutelage under Bonebag and Jones where one mistake earned a cuff.

A bell rang up on deck. Even in the storm, David could hear the thunder of feet as the watch was changed.

'They'll be at the hatch in a moment,' said Sally, throwing open the upper half of the cabin door. 'You can help me serve.'

David peered out from behind Sally into the squally darkness. Dark figures wrapped in oilskins were converging on the hatch. With brief words of thanks, they took their ration and disappeared below decks to eat. By the time they had served the last hungry sailor, David noticed that the wind had dropped and the sea had ceased to break furiously across the decks. The motion of the ship was far more violent than he would normally consider comfortable, but in comparison to the storm they had just endured it was nothing.

'Time for our own breakfast,' said Sally closing the hatch and taking down two stools from their place lashed to the wall.

'But I've given away the last rasher,' said David miserably.

'Fortunately for you, my young apprentice, I know better than that. Cook's privilege: a little of the best of everything.' She fumbled in the stove and pulled out a pan of eggs and bacon that she had been keeping warm. 'Tuck in.'

They were chatting happily together, talking about Earth, about their memories of other meals on dry land, when there came a sharp rap at the door. Sally put her fork down.

'I've been expecting this,' she said, hurrying to open it. 'Is it time?' she asked the slim, dark figure.

'The boy's to come with me,' said Mia with a nod.

'Then I'll come too,' said Sally, pulling her cloak back on. 'Get under here, sonny.'

Reluctantly, David left the warmth of the kitchen and was smuggled across the rain-washed deck to the captain's cabin. Mia knocked once and led them straight in.

'Where's the boy?' said a deep-toned voice. 'I thought I asked you to bring him. Are yet more of my orders to be ignored?'

Sally pushed David out from under her cloak.

'He's here, Captain,' she said boldly.

David stared across the cabin into the eyes of the most beautiful creature he had ever seen. Reports of Captain Tor's beauty had failed to capture the shimmer of gold that hung around her glowing skin, her ash-silver hair, or high arched eyebrows. *Could this creature possibly turn into something as hideous as Mother Reckland?* David wondered.

'I should've guessed,' smiled Stella Tor sourly, 'that you'd have a man clinging to your skirts. You always liked them too much, Sally: that was your downfall.'

'Don't I know it, ma'am, but this one's just a boy.'

'But in case you haven't noticed, boys like him grow up into men like Captain Fisher.'

'Not on the Seas In-between, they don't,' replied Sally smartly. 'He'll stay a boy for ever if he remains here.'

Tor smiled, amused by her crewman's answer. 'You almost make me forgive you, Sally. But it's no good: he'll have to go.'

'At least take him back to Earth,' pleaded Sally.

Captain Tor whipped something out from her belt and threw it across the cabin at the cook. Sally ducked. David stood open-mouthed when he realized there was an emerald-studded dagger quivering in the wall behind him.

'No, not a moment longer. I will not have my ship sullied by his presence!' Tor shrieked.

David couldn't believe it: he was about to be pitched over the side of another ship—this time just because he was a boy. And Milli—she'd risked so much for him!

'At least keep my parrot,' he blurted out. 'She's a girl—you'll not mind her.'

His words jolted Tor out of her anger like a dash of cold water in the face.

'You plead for your parrot and not for yourself?' she marvelled, looking into his face.

'See, Captain, he's not a man yet. He still thinks of others first,' Sally chipped in, seeing her chance to widen the chink of interest David's bravery had opened.

'He doesn't look much like a man,' agreed Tor, running her long fingernail over his smooth chin and freckled face.

'No indeed, he's almost as pretty as a girl, ain't he, ma'am. No belching—no swearing—no coarse manners,' Sally lied.

Hmm.' Tor walked away from David and levered her knife out of the wall. 'Tell me your tale, child, and I'll tell you if you can stay.'

Nervously, hands clasped behind his back, David told the story of his marooning and 'rescue' by the *Scythe*. He didn't dare look at Tor, instead focusing on the rich blue carpet of her cabin.

'Come here, child,' said Captain Tor, beckoning him to her side. He barely reached her shoulder— that seemed to please her. 'You've been through a lot for one so young. Why?'

David told her the truth. 'To save my friends; to save the worlds.'

'Selfless—how rare it is to find this quality in a creature. You're right, Sally, this boy is no man or he would not think like this. Men are weak; men are greedy.'

David couldn't let this pass. 'Not all men, ma'am,' he said respectfully. 'Not Captain Fisher and his crew. They're trying to save the worlds too.'

'Don't speak to me of that man!' Tor exploded again. David realized too late he had been stupid to open his mouth. Her moods were as

184

unpredictable as the gusts of wind in a storm. 'He deludes himself. He's just after the treasure of others. He wants to deprive us all of our comforts!'

'He doesn't keep them for himself,' muttered David defiantly.

A hand gripped his hair and wrenched his head back so that he was now looking straight up into the harsh green eyes.

'Say that again, boy, and you die!'

David could hear Sally clucking anxiously in the background.

'But it's the truth. I've seen it for myself,' he persisted.

Tor let go of him and pushed him roughly away. David fell, colliding with the edge of the table and his lip split. Anger flared up inside him. He was sick of being pushed around!

'He stole from me too, you know,' he spoke to her back as he wiped the blood from his chin. 'He stole my greatest treasure—something I made with my own hands—but I don't hold it against him!'

Stella Tor was striding away. David felt sure she was about to give the order that he be thrown overboard.

'Don't you understand that there are some things worth more than gold or treasure?' he cried out desperately. 'Worth more than even your own life? I've risked my life to help Captain Fisher, but what have you risked? Nothing: you're still sulking over a bit of gold he took from you. But maybe, just maybe, that's the gold that has stopped Tarnis disappearing off into the Inferno Rim, have you ever thought of that?'

Tor swung round, her eyes blazing. Sally swooped down on David and put her hand over his mouth to stop him saying any more.

'Let him speak, Crewman,' barked Tor. 'You, you dare to preach to me, little boy!' she said bearing down on David like a lioness coming in for the kill. 'I could have you thrown overboard with a click of my fingers! I could hand you back to Jones and watch him lash you to death!'

'You could and I wouldn't care,' David said recklessly. Words tumbled out of him—words he didn't know till then were waiting to escape. He'd had enough of bullies, enough of people who didn't stop to help when someone was so plainly in trouble. 'At least, I know that I'm doing the right thing. Do *you* know that? When have you ever helped anyone? Where were you when Tintel disappeared beyond reach? Were you cutting the threads or crying for your lost gold? Can't you help the *Needle* for once— help me?'

Tor raised her hand to strike him but David stared her down.

'Go on, do it! Hit me if it'll make you feel better. But it won't, I can tell you that now for nothing. You're twisted, you are—you with your females-only thing—your sulking over a treasure long since gone.'

'It's not the treasure,' she spat.

'What is it then? It seems to me you should stop sitting on the fence—stop pretending the struggle between the *Needle* and the *Scythe* is nothing to do with you. Take me back to Fisher. Help us stop Jones. Maybe then you'll feel better.'

David took a deep breath. He knew he'd gone way too far now, but he did not care.

Tor was silent for a moment, staring at David with mingled wonder and loathing.

'I met a man like you not long ago,' she said, a bitter smile on her red lips, 'all washed up on Carl. He tried to convince us to cut the threads so that Carl and Earth would drift into the Inferno Rim. He told us it was the only way to save the other worlds from the pirates.'

'Who was he? Where was he?' asked David.

'We left him on Carl. I refused him passage out. I expect he's still there, snipping away on his mad quest, haunting the Carlians like a ghost.'

'He's not mad,' David said, realization dawning. 'He's right. If the *Scythe* can't reach engine parts or oil, the *Needle* stands a chance. The other worlds will be safe. The *Golden Needle* will be able to sew them as she did in the past.'

Her revelation left him reeling. Though relieved that his father was not cutting the thread for gain, David had not yet got over the shock that, by the sound of it, he was prepared to sacrifice Earth, and doom his own family, to save the other worlds. But then, if nothing was done, the worlds would all be doomed in any case. He was only speeding things up.

'Look, please take me back to the *Needle*, I beg you,' David continued. 'Think of me as mad, I don't care, but take me to Fisher.'

Tor said nothing. She scrutinized him coldly. David's pleas weren't working.

'Even you must care for something,' David suggested. 'Don't you care what will happen to Tarnis? Don't you want to get back home some day?'

Tor shrugged. 'Why should I care about Tarnis? If I go there, I'll quickly grow old and ugly. At least here, I have perpetual youth— almost.'

Sally stirred restlessly.

'Even you will get old one day—unless you

settle for sitting in the middle of the starlit seas,' David persisted.

Sally nodded. 'He's right, ma'am. We should help.'

Tor dug her jewelled knife onto the table. David noticed then that the back of her right hand had a light frosting of scales tinged with grey.

'All right, all right, I'll take him to his damned ship,' she said furiously. 'Now, get out.'

CHAPTER THIRTEEN
Cutting the Threads

'Well, that didn't go too bad now, did it?' chuckled Sally as she prepared the noon meal.

David was sitting in the corner with Michael, feeling miserable.

'You're joking?' he muttered.

'No, I'm not,' said Sally, throwing some onions into a pan and stirring them as they hissed in the hot oil. 'You got your way with the captain: there's few that can say that much. My money was on you ending up in the rowing boat with a flask of water and a bag of biscuit. Instead, we are carrying you like some little prince back to his kingdom. There's more of Tiberius Jones in you than you realize, sonny.'

David winced. He had felt a wild, reckless anger boil up inside him when confronted by the selfishness of Stella Tor, that was true, but that didn't make him like Jones, surely?

'Ah, I remember Tiberius as a lad. He was full of big ideas like you. Went to sea to help his poor old mother, he did, after she had a fall and could no longer keep the family with her wages. He was a good boy—loyal, honest, kind when he could be. I might've done better falling for him than his rapscallion friend, Reuben Fisher.' She added some garlic to the pot as it sizzled away.

'It was Reuben that turned him, you might say,' continued Sally. 'Gave him a taste for the finer things in life—including the bottle.' She dug into her apron pocket and took a swig from a hip flask. 'You have to have money for that kind of life and you won't always come by that by being a good little boy now, will you? With daring you can make that bit extra. But in my experience daring soon becomes not caring—not caring for your own life or that of others. Yes, they were a terrible twosome, Shark Fisher and Tiberius Jones.'

This story only served to deepen David's melancholy. It was easier to think of Jones as an out-and-out villain. To understand that he had shades to his character made hating him more difficult.

'What do you think, Sally? Should I have tried harder to argue him out of his pirate ways?' David asked.

'Ach, sonny, there's naught you can do about an old dyed-in-the-wool rogue like Jones. If he's to change, he'll have to do the changing himself—like old Shark has. Now let me tell you something more cheerful.'

Sally began to regale him with tales of the Seas In-between drawn from her many years wandering these waters.

'Have you seen the lightning?' she asked David. He shook his head. 'Well, when it strikes the water, it gives birth to shoals of electric blue fish that sting you if you so much as touch them. You can see them from afar like great stripes of summer sky come down to rest in the waters, but you must keep away or they'll fry you like these onions.'

She took a cleaver to a leg of lamb and threw chunks over her shoulder—each one plopping perfectly into the pot without her turning around.

'And there are the twisters. Mighty storms that can swallow a ship in one gulp and take them down to the worlds below.'

'Worlds below?' David said in wonder. 'You mean there are more worlds still—worlds beneath the sea?'

'Yes—or so they say. Mia swears she glimpsed the top of one of their mountains during a storm many years ago, but I didn't see it myself.'

Sally smiled at David's frank look of wide-eyed wonder.

'And then there's the mermaids—beautiful creatures with long green hair and shell-white skin.'

'Mermaids? There are mermaids too?'

Sally went off into a peal of laughter. When she had recovered and wiped her eyes on her apron, she said: 'Not really, sonny. But you seemed to be enjoying yourself so much hearing my silly tales that I just couldn't resist slipping in a bit of embroidery to see if you noticed.'

David felt grumpy with her for pulling his leg. How was he to know what was true and false out here?

'And the lightning—the worlds?' he asked.

'They're as real as you and me, David,' she said, looking serious now. 'You'll never stop seeing wonders if you stay here on the Seas In-between; but something tells me you are bound for port, am I right?'

David nodded. 'I must finish my task, find my dad—he's out here too somewhere—and get home if I can.'

'Ah,' said Sally, coming to sit on Michael to rest her tired legs. 'I sometimes think it would be nice to have a home again. Perhaps I should stop wandering too, but I'm not sure I'd know how. I've been doing it that long. Well, sonny, I'm going to turn in for a bit of shut-eye while the stew cooks. Keep an eye on it for me?'

David was left alone in the galley to his thoughts, hypnotized by the steady swaying to and fro of a string of onions on the ceiling beam. His mind kept circling back to his father cutting the threads on Carl. Two worlds with the supplies to keep the *Scythe*'s engines running to be cast adrift to save the others—David could see that this was a reasonable price to pay if you considered all the people that would be saved, but his heart did not want to accept it. He wished someone would blow the *Scythe* out of the water instead and solve the problem that way, but she was so much more powerful than either the *Wanderer* or the *Needle* that there seemed no prospect of that. Whatever happened, he wanted to be with his people if the threads were cut; he would prefer to be back home facing the end with his mother and grandad than bobbing about unscathed out here while they suffered.

By evening the lookout had spotted the trail of the *Golden Needle* twinkling in the sunshine. The next morning, David could see the familiar sails to starboard with the naked eye. A signal was run up the mast and the two great ships tacked to converge on each other. David hung eagerly over the side as a boat was sent to fetch him. Captain Fisher was again at the oars, this time accompanied by Shushula.

'Davy!' squealed the cabin girl the moment her feet hit the deck. She hugged him as tightly as her thin arms would allow. 'We feared you were dead—or worse.'

'I was,' smiled David, ruffling her silver hair, 'but your present saved me.'

Captain Fisher climbed over the rail and bowed low to Stella Tor.

'Charmed to meet you as always, Captain,' he said respectfully. 'But this time, I must add my heartfelt thanks for restoring a member of my crew to me.'

Stella stared at him, anger flickering in her eyes. David wondered for a moment if her rage would flare out like the lightning Sally had told him about and strike Fisher down.

'The sooner you both depart, the better,' she said tersely.

'Of course, as you command. Dare I invite you to dine with me, ma'am, as token of my thanks?'

'You dare too far, Fisher. I'd rather eat with the frapgins than with you,' she replied.

'Of course, ma'am. I understand from the boy here that they are very good company.' He winked at David.

The crew of the *Needle* was assembled in ranks as David was pushed up first over the side, Milli perched on his shoulder. He thought for a chilling moment of his last minutes on the *Scythe*, but then the sailors broke into three cheers. Those with caps threw them in the air. Art hopped forward and surprised David by enfolding him in a sweaty hug.

'Glad to see you back, boy,' he said.

Ruramina, the tall tiger-skinned second mate, sauntered to his side and stroked his salt-matted locks.

'Thank you,' she purred. 'You have more than fulfilled our expectations.'

David shivered at her touch, feeling as if she had just tickled him with a feather.

Fisher strode forward.

'Davy, let's go to my cabin and hear your news.'

Shushula, Art, and Ruramina followed the captain as he led David to his quarters. Jemima squawked indignantly when she saw her only chick arrive with the party.

'Peace, you old termagant,' crooned Captain Fisher. 'You're to be friends now.'

Huffily, Jemima made room for Milli on her perch and offered her the second best nut in her collection.

'So, Davy, tell us what you know,' said Fisher, putting his fingertips together as he sat to listen to the boy's tale.

David told them all about the engines, the raid on Carl, his sabotage, walking the plank and his rescue.

Fisher gave a whistle between his teeth, his gold fangs glinting.

'You were born lucky, Davy,' he said.

David wasn't sure if he would have called being whipped and made to walk the plank 'lucky' but he supposed his survival was nothing short of a miracle.

'So Jones has special devices called "engines",' said Fisher thoughtfully. 'Sound like the work of the devil to me. What do they do?'

'They're sort of a bit like metal sails that don't need wind, always ready to move the ship along at any speed the captain wants.'

Fisher frowned. 'But you said you damaged them. How long till they're mended?'

'That depends on Farthing. He's the only one who really understands engines. They are from his era on Earth. He'll need to get spare parts and that will be difficult. They'll have to raid some museum in my time.'

'So, they'll be heading for Earth.'

'Not immediately. They have to repair their mast first.'

Fisher stroked his chin thoughtfully. 'Good, that gives us time to think up a plan to stop them.'

'There is something we can do,' added David heavily. 'In fact, according to Captain Tor, some-one's already doing it.' He went on to tell them about his father cutting the threads binding Earth and Carl to the other worlds.

Strangely, the story made Fisher smile. 'So there's another Jones out there, is there? You think one's enough and then three come along together.'

'But you've got to stop him,' protested Art. 'He's condemning my people—and yours—to certain death!'

'It might not come to that. There are more ways than one to skin a cat. Sorry, Ruramina,' Fisher added hastily as his second mate growled in her throat. 'Leave it with me.'

Back out on deck, Shushula scampered lightly to his side.

'I'm so pleased to have you back,' she said, stroking his arm. 'You've been so brave. I can't tell you how proud of you we all are. You've done much to redeem the name of Jones on the Seas In-between.'

David sighed. 'You all know, don't you, what the captain thinks?'

Shushula nodded. 'Yes, he told us that you had Jones blood in your veins after we saw you shooting at us. He guessed that Jones had forced you to do it. He told us you couldn't help it.' There was a note in her voice that did not sound quite right: she was hiding something.

'He didn't say that really, did he?' said David.

She grimaced. Er . . . no. Not at first. He said you were a no-good traitor like your relative and that we should never have trusted you. He calmed down later after Art and I persuaded him that you'd've had no choice.'

David laughed bitterly. 'To tell you the truth, I rather enjoyed smashing his windows. You should've heard what he said about me to Jones.'

'I know, Davy, which is why he's now even prouder of you. You stuck to your purpose even in the face of real doubt and fear. It takes a fine person to do that.'

There was a heavy tread behind them. David turned to see Captain Fisher standing there, his plumed hat framed against the pale twinkle of the stars as the *Golden Needle* sailed once more into the starlit seas.

'Can I have a moment with Davy, Shushula?' Fisher asked quietly.

Shushula got up and went to join the rest of the crew.

'Come with me, lad,' said Fisher.

They walked to the poop deck, which was deserted except for the man dozing at the wheel. A white bird circled overhead, looping the masts.

'I want to apologize to you, Davy, for putting you through that ordeal. I knew, of course, when I left you on that island, that you'd suffer.'

David stared out over the inky waves to the lights of the *Wanderer* sailing gently alongside them a stone's cast away.

'And do you know what, Davy, though it was a good plan, perhaps the only plan open to us, it was made easier for me because I fear I didn't really care what happened to you. You see, Jones was right about me in one thing. I'm not a saint—I'm a sinner. Seeing your face reawakened a ruthless streak in me. I risked a boy to save the rest of us. That's not right. It shows I've still a long way to go.'

Fisher sighed and put his arm around David's shoulders. 'And do you know something else? I realized I was jealous when I saw you with Jones, yes, even when he was helping you take a pot shot at me. What lonely old men we both are! I spoke with real anger when we met in the boats—useful to continue the deception, we both know, but hard for you to hear. But you've proved yourself to me.' He paused. 'You've become dear to me. I'd like you to stay.'

David was choked with emotion. Fisher's words made him feel taller. He felt how he did when his father was there to cheer him on at Sports Day, or when his mother said something nice about him in his hearing.

'Thank you, sir,' he said quietly, smiling at the darkness and enjoying the weight of the captain's arm on his shoulder. At that moment, David felt as if he could spend the rest of his days on the Seas In-between with his new family.

'So, that is why it pains me to have to let you go, Davy. For I know I must.'

David started to protest, his happy mood punctured.

'No, my boy, we've both been called on to make a sacrifice to save the worlds. You are mine,' said Captain Fisher solemnly.

'Sacrifice?' David didn't like the sound of this.

'You'll see.' Fisher dropped his arm, the time for intimacies had passed. 'Enjoy the celebrations tonight. We've many difficult days ahead.'

He strode away to nudge the man at the wheel awake. David watched him go, torn between feelings of admiration and distrust. He had almost believed Fisher then, almost been persuaded that the captain did indeed care for him, but this talk of sacrifice had capsized that dream.

Early the next day they made landfall on Carl. David watched with horrified fascination as the *Golden Needle* sailed along the coast, snipping the golden threads of her past voyages. Some threads had already been cut and were found trailing in the water like gilded seaweed. Fisher ordered them to be reeled in.

'I'm not going to leave it here for Jones to find,' he told the team of sailors deployed in the task.

David scanned the coast for his father, but the shoreline was barren of two-legged creatures, except for some long-legged wading birds fishing in the pools. He had begged to be allowed ashore but Fisher said there was no time for a search party. He needed David with him.

'We're bound for the final reckoning, Davy, the day when we settle our scores and risk all to save the worlds. You still have a part to play. Your father would understand,' he said confidently.

At four bells Captain Fisher summoned the

crew on deck. Art was standing by his side with a bundle of belongings under his arm.

'You know what to do?' Fisher said to his first mate.

Art nodded.

David watched as Fisher handed Art a pair of diamond-edged scissors, which the Carlian tucked into his waistband. As the ship tacked into port, Art bade farewell to each of his comrades in turn.

'You're leaving?' David asked him in confusion when his turn arrived.

'Aye, Davy. It's been an honour to serve with you, if but briefly,' said Art, his wrinkled face pinched with sadness as he took a final look around the ship that had been his home for more years than he could remember.

'You're going back home?'

'Nay, lad, I've no home on Carl now. There's no one alive that remembers me. I'm going to disappear among my grandchildren's grand-children for my last tour of duty.' He patted Davy on the back. 'Don't leave it too long to go home. Time has a funny habit of leaving you behind out here.'

Finally, the captain handed Art the thread of the present voyage and led him to the side. Some in the crew took out little pipes and began to play a high shrill note as Art bounded over the side.

With a salute, he disappeared into the mist, pulling a streamer of gold after him.

Fisher turned to see David staring bewildered at the shadowy trees of Carl.

'It only takes one thread,' Fisher said as he strode past. 'Set a course for the last known position of the *Scythe*,' he called to Ruramina.

David gulped.

'What! You mean you are actually seeking Jones out? But why?' The captain's words about sacrifice came back to haunt him.

'Trust me, Davy. I know what I'm doing. We're going to settle this once and for all, one way or another.'

CHAPTER FOURTEEN
Sacrifice

Shushula was teaching David how to fish with a rod when the *Scythe* was spotted. David almost dropped it into the water on hearing the cry from the crow's nest.

'Are we going to clear the decks for action?' asked David.

Shushula was squinting up at a row of flags that had just been run up the mast.

'No,' she said, biting her lip. 'We're to meet the *Scythe* at Wreckers Island. He's challenged Jones to a duel.'

'Where's the island?' David asked, wondering how much time was left.

'It's not far—near landfall for your world. What's really going on? Do you know? I thought perhaps the captain might have told you last night.'

David shook his head. 'All he said is that we have to make a sacrifice.'

'What kind of sacrifice?'

'That's what I'd like to know.' He didn't add that it was something to do with him or give voice to the fear that he was a bargaining chip in this game of Fisher's.

The voyage to Wreckers Island was a strange time for David. He spent many hours watching the *Needle* cut its own threads binding Earth to the Seas In-between, rolling in the gold before the *Scythe* could catch up with them.

'Jones won't be pleased,' muttered Shushula as another heavy bobbin of gold was stored away below. 'We're doing his work for him.'

'That's it!' cried Captain Fisher, checking his chart. 'That's the last thread. Earth is free of its bonds and will begin to drift.'

He seemed very pleased with the news that he had just condemned his home to the Inferno Rim. David and Shushula exchanged worried glances. David thought he knew why it was being done: Fisher was putting his world beyond the reach of the *Scythe*. But, in that case, why had Fisher left Carl connected by Art's thread? None of it made sense.

Wreckers Island appeared to starboard, crouching like the spiny back of a dragon in the blue seas. Fisher ordered the *Golden Needle* to moor in a bay sheltered by a steep headland.

'Prepare the boat!' commanded the captain. 'David, Shushula, Halist, Ruramina—with me.'

David saw that Ruramina was strapping on a curved cutlass and Halist was sniffing the powder of his pistol to check it was dry before he put the handle in his mouth.

'Will Jones come, do you think?' David asked Shushula, watching the *Scythe* nervously.

She nodded. 'I don't think Captain Jones will be able to resist the temptation to fight. He could get the *Needle* without a spar of her being harmed.'

'Look lively, you two!' bellowed Captain Fisher spotting the two smallest members of his crew hovering on the deck.

David felt Shushula take his hand and give it a squeeze.

'Don't worry, Davy, you can trust him. He'll fight for us all of us. Let's go.'

They jumped into the boat together. Milli flew from the rigging to settle on her favourite perch on David's shoulder.

Ruramina took the oars. Halist slithered to the prow, his gold crest alert, looking like the figurehead of a sea serpent on a Viking longboat. Fisher sat in the stern, honing the edge of a sword with the regular scrape of metal on whetting stone. He caught David's eye.

'What do you think, Davy? Finest Spanish steel,' he said, holding the blade up to the light where it shone with icy fire.

David felt a lump in his throat. The last time he'd been this close to a cutlass it had been prodding him in the back.

'Very nice, sir,' he said hoarsely. 'Though, to be honest, I don't like being this close to a sword.'

'You're a sensible boy. For them that don't know how to use them, they spell trouble. However, there's many a time this little beauty stood between me and my death,' said Fisher, returning it to its scabbard with a clunk.

The flat-bottomed rowing boat made its way carefully between the teeth of rocks that ringed the island. In the shallows, Fisher and David jumped out to pull the boat onto the sandy beach.

'Where's the meeting place?' asked Ruramina as they stowed the boat above the high-water mark.

'On the crown of Skull Hill,' said Fisher.

'How will Jones know?' she enquired, gazing out to sea at the approaching sails of the *Scythe*.

'He'll know. It's where many years ago I persuaded him forcefully to leave my crew.'

Fisher led the way, cutting a path through the brambles that festooned the cliffs on this island. Only the seabirds visited it now, leaving white marks on all the cliff edges. David noticed a little bird with a multicoloured beak dive off a ledge, leaving a blue egg unprotected on its perilous perch. He could hear the distant clamour of a large bird colony around the next headland. Milli screeched a reply, but resisted the temptation to go off to explore.

Fisher continued climbing, his shoulders hunched with the exertion. The sun was hot on the back of David's neck and sweat dripped from the end of his nose. Shushula stumbled beside him, stopped from falling by the swift paw of Ruramina. Only Halist seemed unaffected as he slithered up the burning rocks. They reached the top of the hill, a bald platform giving sweeping views in all directions. On the horizon David could see the line of mist that hid the ports on Earth. The sky overhead was a deep blue. Down below them, the *Scythe* slid into the bay and furled her sails, mooring not quite in cannon-shot of her rival. In the middle distance, a white shape moved rapidly across the turquoise seas, heading in their direction. Fisher took out his telescope.

'Interesting,' he murmured to himself as he gazed at the approaching sail. 'Very interesting.'

He shut his telescope with a snap and turned to his crewmen.

'I'm expecting some visitors. Let us make ourselves comfortable while they endure the hot climb.'

He spread his jacket over a rock and sat down, fanning himself with his hat. Hesitating for a second, his crewmen followed his example. There was no shade. David put his waistcoat over his and Shushula's head, improvising a little tent for them both.

Heavy breathing and loud curses preceded the arrival of Jones and his deputation. Up onto the brow of the rock came the captain, followed by Bonebag, Farthing, and Vorgat. The Tarnisian was carrying a wooden box containing Captain Jones's pistols.

'Delighted you could make it,' said Fisher, jumping to his feet. 'Do make yourselves at home and catch your breath.' He had his hand to his cutlass for all his polite words.

Jones looked around him, his eyes resting for a startled moment on David. Farthing too looked horrified to see him there.

'You!' Jones spat, taking a step towards David, hand raised to strike. Milli squawked in protest.

Fisher quickly stepped in between them.

'A useful bit of jetsam, as you once commented, Tiberius,' he said lightly.

'He should be dead. He will be, if I have anything to do with it,' growled Jones, his fists now balled at his side.

'Quite so. But first things first. What say you to this challenge of mine?'

'Challenge?'

'A duel. You against me—as it should've been years ago.'

Tiberius unclenched his fists and stood back from Fisher, looking him up and down.

'What, no tricks?'

'No tricks,' agreed Fisher.

'And the stake?'

'If you win, you get the gold—all of it—and the *Golden Needle* too. You can appoint a captain to your own liking.'

Farthing stirred at Jones's side, his interest aroused by the talk of a command becoming vacant.

'And the boy? I get my kinsman to roast slowly over a fire?' Jones spat at David's feet, his spittle hissing on the hot rocks.

Fisher bowed. 'Of course. I doubt I'll be here to stop you, will I? Neither Davy nor I expect mercy from you. You can sacrifice him to your greed for revenge if you must.'

David swallowed, his throat as dry and rough as sandpaper. There was Fisher's streak of ruthlessness again, ready to damn himself and his cabin boy all in the single-minded determination to save the worlds.

Shushula clung close to him.

'He won't let that happen,' she whispered.

'You want a bet?' David replied, meeting her eyes.

She dropped her gaze.

'And what if you win?' Jones asked his enemy slyly.

'Assuming I don't kill you—' Fisher gave a wicked grin, flashing his gold teeth, '—then you'll be bound by your word as a pirate never again to cut the bonds binding the other worlds to the Seas In-between.'

'So little?'

'That's all I demand. But I should warn you, I hold your source of fuel and spare parts to ransom. Earth and Carl will each be bound by a single thread to the other worlds on the Seas In-between. If you break your word and cut a thread, I will send a message to my watchmen. They will sever the bonds of Earth and Carl, preventing you from ever reaching them again, crippling the *Scythe* for good.'

Jones strode to the cliff edge, gazing out at the hazy outline of Earth on the horizon.

212

'Why should I care about that? It'll take Earth and Carl a long while to sail out of my reach—plenty of time for me to lay up stocks elsewhere, or even live out my days somewhere on Earth if I so choose.'

'Are you so sure of that?' Fisher gestured to the sun burning overhead. 'We're near Earth now and your skin tells you the air is scorching. Our world is already on the edge of the Inferno Rim. Remember Tintel? Once the currents of the Rim took hold, there was no stopping a world's demise. Tintel sailed out of reach so fast, I could do nothing about it. All I could save was one girl on a melting icefloe.'

Jones scowled and wiped the sweat from his brow.

'Think about it, Tiberius. If you win, you have a chance to lay your hands on more gold than you have ever dreamed of.'

'Don't you believe it, Shark,' snarled Jones. 'My dreams are beyond your limited imagination. I dream of seas of gold—not even the *Needle* and all her cargo will satisfy them.'

'But it would be a start, I've no doubt,' smiled Fisher. 'What do you say?'

He got no answer immediately for there was a noise of more people approaching the summit of the hill. David spun round quickly, fearing some surprise attack by Jones's crew. He was astonished to see Stella Tor, shaded by an immense pink silk parasol, climbing the steep path from the cove, closely followed by a scarlet-faced Sally Ann Bowers. Down on the water, a third ship had moored between the *Scythe* and the *Needle*, in a position between the two vessels to prevent any broadside should either crew contemplate mounting an attack in their captain's absence.

Captain Fisher was the only one who did not seem surprised to see her.

'My dear Captain, you are most welcome to this reunion of old friends,' he declared, gallantly waving her to the rock he had covered with his own jacket.

Stella Tor sat down and planted the parasol beside her.

'Friends, Captain Fisher?' she asked wryly. 'Then why the swords and pistols?'

'That's because, as old friends, Tiberius and I know each other too well to come unarmed.'

Jones had now recovered from his surprise and made a deep bow.

'Ma'am, your presence honours us,' he said, hand on his heart.

'Captain Jones, it's been too long,' Stella said with a tolerant smile at her admirer. 'Not that I haven't had news of you. You were so kind as to send me a message in the shape of that boy there'—she gestured to David—'letting me know that you were still up to your old ways.'

Jones wasn't sure if this was a criticism and gave her an apologetic smile.

'A most scurvy dog, ma'am, I'm sorry if he troubled you,' he said. 'You should've left him for the sharks as I intended.'

'I would've done, had I had anything to do with it, but the hearts of some females I know are too easily swayed by pity.' She cast a sidelong look at Sally, who returned her gaze unabashed.

'At least I have a heart to be touched,' muttered Sally.

'Well, ma'am, I am pleased to say that none of my crew suffers from that weakness,' said Jones. 'When I win this duel, you'll have the pleasure of seeing the boy's long delayed punishment being carried out.'

'A duel?' mused Stella, her beautiful eyes flicking speculatively from Fisher to Jones. 'So, that is what this is all about.'

'And your arrival is most timely, ma'am,' said Fisher. 'If you would condescend to be the referee, we will both rest assured that fair play will be observed.'

'Fair play?' laughed Stella Tor mockingly. 'When did you ever play fair, Fisher?' She flicked her long ash-silver hair over her shoulder, revealing a white scar on her bare arm.

He acknowledged her reproof with a bow.

'There must be a start to everything, Captain.'

Stella Tor stood up and placed her hands on her hips.

'I accept the role assigned to me. I will find it highly amusing to see you two billy goats butting each other. So, what's it to be: swords or pistols?'

'Pistols, sir,' Farthing muttered to Jones, drawing from his pocket a dull metal gun that looked suspiciously like a revolver, far more deadly than the single-shot pistols that Vorgat had lugged up the hill.

'Swords, of course,' said Fisher with a glance at the revolver. 'They were the weapons that started Tiberius and me on our course to piracy, so they should finish it.'

Jones nodded and pushed Farthing away. He drew from his side the cutlass that he had used to prod David overboard. It glittered in the blinding sunlight as if the blade were made of molten metal.

'Swords it is. I'm surprised, Shark: you know I'm a better hand at the blade than you; whereas your aim with the barking irons was always truer.' He threw off his jacket to stand in his shirtsleeves, his crimson waistcoat gleaming like fresh blood.

216

'Time changes many things, Tiberius. It's long since we've measured swords together.' Fisher threw his hat to Ruramina and unsheathed his own blade.

Jones took a couple of preparatory swipes at the air, the edge of the sword whistling as it went.

'Do you remember that sea-captain you filleted in Jamaica, Shark, the one who looked at you oddly—or so you said.'

'Aye, every day,' said Fisher, standing still as his rival danced about him.

'Paid your dues for him yet?' mocked Jones.

'No, but at least I've made a beginning. Your bill has doubled since.'

'Don't try and scare me with your preaching, Shark. You are up to your elbows in blood: no amount of stitching can wash that away.'

'Now, gentlemen,' said Stella Tor, stepping between them. 'Are you ready?'

Both raised their blades.

'Aye,' they intoned.

'Is this to first blood or to the death?' she asked them.

'To the death,' said Jones quickly.

'I'd be content with first blood,' replied Fisher.

'May fortune favour the brave!' she declared. 'Begin.'

Leaping back, she made way for the two combatants. Like a Rottweiler let off the leash, Jones dashed forward eagerly, driving Fisher backwards with a rain of deadly blows that he had to parry furiously, forced onto his back foot. As David watched his captain struggling, he felt increasingly desperate. Fisher did indeed seem the less skilled swordsman, which meant death for both of them. Milli's pert crest drooped in sympathy.

Farthing sidled over to David, his eyes on the battle but his mouth employed with blood-curdling threats.

'Do you know, dog boy, you'll soon be begging us to throw you to the sharks. You won't get off so lightly this time. No quick death for you. First, we're going to flog you until your bones show. We'll all take a turn—nice and slow—I can't tell you how much the crew will enjoy it. I imagine it'll take us about a week. When you're crawling on your hands and knees to beg us to put you out of your misery, then maybe we'll shut you in a box with a hungry frapgin. If you scream loud enough, we may finally tip you over the side to try your luck with those sharks. You've not seen the sharks of the Seas In-between, have you? They make the sharks of our world look like minnows.'

David could feel cold sweat trickling down his back. Fisher had just stumbled over a stone and was fighting on one knee.

'Shut up, you pale-faced toad,' hissed Shushula. 'If you harm my friend, I'll dig your eyes out with my fingernails.'

She flexed her long, thin, and extremely sharp-looking fingers at him. Farthing fell silent, but gave her an evil glare.

Now Jones's eyes were glinting with triumph as he pushed his advantage over Fisher, taking great swipes at him as if he meant to sever his head from his body with one cut. Fisher ducked one swinging blow, sending Jones staggering off balance. He leapt to his feet and kicked Jones in the rear. The pirate went flying, his blade arcing out of his hand to clatter at Stella Tor's feet, the sword of his adversary now between his shoulder blades.

Wiping beads of sweat from his brow, Fisher gasped: 'That was always your weakness, Tiberius, showmanship over strategy.' He nicked the pirate on the cheek, drawing first blood. 'Do you yield?'

Jones, his mouth full of dust, had no chance to reply for just then a shot rang out. Milli screeched and flapped into the air in alarm. Fisher gave a cry and fell to the ground clutching his shoulder.

David spun round to see Farthing aiming his revolver for a second shot.

'Take it from me, Fisher, the captain doesn't yield to anyone,' said Farthing.

'No!' David leapt on the arm holding the gun, forcing the barrel to point to the floor. He felt the recoil as the bullet hit the dirt.

'You cheating, lying maggot!' screamed Shushula, throwing herself at Farthing, leaving the trail of her nails down his cheek. Farthing couldn't shake her off as he was battling with David. Bonebag weighed in and gripped David's wrists, forcing him to release his hold on Farthing's arm. David kicked the Dammian in the stomach and twisted free, diving out of reach behind Halist. Meanwhile, Farthing had grabbed Shushula and pulled her off his back. He now caught her neck in an armlock and put the revolver to her temple. Everyone froze.

'Good, I see you all understand the language of the bullet,' he said, panting as he surveyed the company. Fisher lay still on the ground, the sand beneath him stained red with his blood. Jones got to his feet and retrieved his fallen sword with a grin. He swiped it at Milli, who flew to Sally to take cover on her shoulder.

'Right, let's get back to the bargaining now our position is a mite stronger,' said Farthing, gloating over the head of the girl he was half-strangling. 'We get the traitor, the ship, and the gold or the girl dies.'

Ruramina growled deep in her throat and put an arm on David's shoulder protectively. Halist hissed like water on hot coals, but Vorgat had the pistols trained on them and a look in his eye that said he needed little encouragement to fire.

'Come, come, Tiger,' said Farthing tutting. 'You can't tell me you'd prefer to save his worthless skin rather than hers?'

David knew he had no choice. He couldn't watch Farthing murder his friend.

'It's all right,' said David, brushing Ruramina's hand away. 'I'll go—if he promises to keep his word and lets her free.' He was horribly aware that every moment spent bargaining meant more of Captain Fisher's blood leaking into the hot earth. They were outnumbered—he would save Shushula and his captain if he could.

Jones, his dignity only partially restored from being kicked in the rear by Fisher, stepped over his rival and seized David by the ear.

'That's right, Davy, you come back to your jolly old uncle. He's got a few party games in mind for you.' He dragged David over to Bonebag who produced handcuffs and leg-irons from his cloak and shackled David.

'No, David!' sobbed Shushula. 'Don't let them take you!'

'It's too late, missy,' crooned Farthing, squeezing her tighter. 'When I'm the new commander of the *Needle*, you'll be shark bait too for your talk of scratching my eyes out. His sacrifice was useless.'

'Farthing, you're a lying wart!' shouted David in outrage. He didn't manage to get another insult out because Vorgat punched him in the stomach, winding him.

'Very good, David,' laughed Farthing. 'I may be a wart, but this wart has the pistol at your dear friend's temple, so I'd cut the smart talk if I were you. She's not got long to live but how would you like to think it was you who shortened her miserable existence?'

It was hopeless. David writhed in the dirt, clutching his stomach, knowing that this was just a taste of what was to come. But then he saw pink leather boots move swiftly to stand behind Farthing. Something glittered green in the air.

'Wrong, baby-face,' said Stella Tor. 'I think that she's going to live to a ripe old age. How do I know it? Feel this? Well, tickling your ribs is nine inches of steel. Let my sister go.'

Farthing's eyes bulged with surprise but he kept the gun clamped to Shushula's head.

'A bit slow are you? I agreed to be here to make sure you played fair, and you, little man, are playing dirty with someone I choose to take under my protection. No girl. No ship. No gold,' she cast a careless look over at David, sprawled on the floor, 'and I suppose, no boy too.'

'My dear Captain,' protested Jones, coming towards her. He had been sure of her as an ally—or at least neutral in this dispute. 'Think what this man and his crew have done to you!'

'I'm not your "dear" anything, Jones, as you should know. And anyway, as someone once told me,' her eyes flicked to David for a second, 'some things are worth more than gold—my honour as a referee and that girl's life being just two of them. Command your boy to drop his gun or I'll give you back your present by sticking it between his ribs.'

Jones's face went dark with anger. He looked down at his rival's bleeding body.

'What care I for one boy? Fisher's done for—I'll take the traitor. You can have Farthing for a pin cushion.'

Stella gave a hearty laugh. 'Think again, Jones, because you'll find that my ship has its guns trained on your decks. If either captain emerges on the beach without my crew receiving my signal, they have orders to sink that man's ship.'

Jones now looked as if someone was strangling him, his eyes popping with rage.

'You'll live to regret this, Stella Tor,' he said, rounding on her with his blade held in front of him. 'You'll regret taking sides. You should've stayed on the fence. Now I'll hunt you down and blow your ship apart.'

'Now, now, Tiberius, don't get your knickers in a twist,' said Sally, drawing a cleaver from her apron pocket and taking aim. 'I think you know I'm a dab hand with the knife, so just you do what my captain tells you and cut the lip, or your lip will be the first thing I cut off with this.'

'Curse you, you pack of old women!' growled Jones, driving his sword into the ground with frustration.

'I'll take that for a "yes",' said Sally, bustling over to Bonebag. 'Here, you useless sack of dog's leavings, undo my boy there or I'll show you just how skilled I am at de-boning a carcass.'

Bonebag eyed the cleaver as he bent down to unlock David's manacles. Sally hauled David to his feet.

'Here, serpent fellow, you and your crewmate should take your captain to your ship. He looks as though he could do with some patching up,' Sally said, gesturing Halist forward.

'He's beyond patching,' Jones said with a bitter laugh. 'At least, that's cause for rejoicing.'

Sally swaggered over to Jones and chucked him under the chin.

'Tiber, sweetheart, I wouldn't be so sure. He's a fighter and a survivor—you know that as well as I.'

'All that remains now, Captain Jones,' said Stella Tor, pricking her dagger deeper into Farthing's back causing him to yelp, 'is to give the order before my little girl here faints. I'll be very angry if she's harmed. It would be worth a broadside at least.'

Jones gave Farthing a curt nod and the boy lowered his revolver, giving his captain a resentful stare. He had not forgiven Jones's readiness to leave him to Stella's dagger. He pushed Shushula away from him so that she fell gasping for breath on the floor. Stella Tor levered the revolver from his grip and then helped Shushula to her feet, brushing her down as tenderly as a mother.

Satisfied the girl was unharmed, Stella turned back to Jones.

'Now we understand each other, I suggest you and your crew wait up here until you see the *Needle* and the *Wanderer* weigh anchor. If I see so much as a whisker of any of you on the beach before we've sailed out of range, I'll fill your boat with so many holes you'll only be able to use it as a sieve.'

Bearing her pink parasol aloft, Stella led the way downhill.

Sally paused in front of Vorgat.

'Now, sonny, you know I never trust boys with toys like these. I think I'll relieve you of them—for your own safety.' She took the pistols, shoved them in her petticoat pocket and followed Halist and Ruramina who had slung Fisher between them. Last of the party, David helped Shushula down the rocky path. As they passed Farthing, the boy took David's arm to hold him back.

'I'll get you!' Farthing hissed. 'You'll never be safe from my revenge. Hide on Earth if you want, but I'll find you there one day.'

'Go to hell,' replied David, shaking him off. 'You and your master deserve each other.'

Captain Jones watched them out of sight but said nothing, his anger beyond words or insults.

'We'd better hurry,' David told Shushula in a low voice. 'This lot will fall on us like a pack of wolves if we lag too far behind. And I doubt Captain Tor will waste a broadside in my defence.'

Shushula gave a faint smile.

'You forget who you're with. She won't let them have me and she might even think you worth a shot or two these days.'

But deciding not to put this to the test, they hurried to catch up with the others.

CHAPTER FIFTEEN

Homeward Bound

Two tall ships sailed up Canal Street, waves of grass breaking against their prows. The *Wanderer*, grey and sleek with spotless white sails, moored on the conservatory of number thirty-three; the *Needle*, multicolour sails and flags flying, beat down the home straight to drop anchor at David's house. Ruramina stood erect at the wheel, her amber eyes fierce with concentration as the ship made a flawless docking.

'Good—very good,' whispered Captain Fisher from his chair at her side. His face was still waxy white and he winced with every slight movement, but Halist's unexpected skill with healing potions had brought him back from death's door. He took a sip of his medicine and grimaced.

'What's it like?' David asked his captain as he stood behind his chair. 'Better or worse than gartan stew?'

The captain thought for a moment and smiled. 'Now you mention it, better.' His shoulders began to heave with laughter. 'Don't make me laugh, Davy, my stitches can't take it yet. You don't want to crack a really side-splitting joke now, do you?'

It was David's turn to smile but this soon faded when he saw his darkened bedroom window and silent house. How was he going to explain his weeks of absence to his mother? Would she ever forgive him?

The crew of the *Wanderer* had lined up along the starboard rail. David could see Sally Ann Bowers, bright in her scarlet petticoat, standing by the cookhouse door, cleaver raised in salute. By her side stood Shushula, sent at her own request and by Captain Fisher's leave, to serve the woman who had saved her life. She waved. David, her lock of hair clenched in his fist, waved back. From the poop deck he thought he caught a fleeting glimpse of a pink jacket, gold skin, and ash-silver hair: so, even Stella Tor had come to bid him farewell. David felt sad at all these partings. It was as if his world was already drifting apart from theirs. They were soon to disappear over a horizon where he would never follow.

'Here, Davy, take these.' Fisher thrust into his hand a gold thread and a pair of diamond-edged scissors. 'You know what you have to do?'

David nodded. 'Cut if I receive the signal from you or if the *Scythe* attacks.'

'That's right. I pray that you'll never need to use them. Find a successor to guard them when your time comes,' added Fisher. 'Any last requests, lad?'

David knew exactly what he wanted—the request had been burning inside him for days. 'If you meet my father, can you bring him back?'

'Aye, we'll send out search parties for him. We don't want him sabotaging our agreement by cutting any more threads, do we now?'

'I would stay and help you look—'

'—But we need you here. This is your post now.' Fisher took a long, last look at his cabin boy. 'I'm proud of you, Davy, proud you redeemed the name of Jones on the Seas In-between. I often think my worst act was to warp Tiberius to my ways when we were lads. I've paid for it since.' He patted his bandaged shoulder. 'But you reminded me painfully of what he could've been if he hadn't met me.'

David shook his head. 'He made his own choices, sir, just as you made yours to change.'

Amused, Fisher cocked an eyebrow. 'Not there yet, am I?'

'Well, there was that bit about leaving me to be roasted over hot coals by the crew of the *Scythe* if you lost the duel.'

Fisher's eyes twinkled. 'In my arrogance, I thought I was going to win. See, I'm still pirate-hearted, despite everything. I've a long way to sail before I can finally give it all up and rest. Well, goodbye, David Jones.' He held out a calloused palm.

'Goodbye, sir.' They shook hands.

'Pipes!'

As Fisher gave the order, shrill whistles broke out from all over the ship, augmented by an answering trill from the *Wanderer*. David shouldered his small pack of belongings gathered on the voyage and shinned over the side, swinging nimbly down to the ground. A grey parrot fluttered down to his shoulder.

'Abandoning ship?' David asked Milli.

She squawked and increased her grip on his shoulder. He turned to look one last time on the *Needle* but it was already fading into the mist that rolled up Waterside. By the time he reached his back door, even the whistle of the pipes had gone. Finding the key under the flowerpot where it always was, he let himself in and closed the door.

* * *

'David!' His mother screamed when she found her lost son sleeping in his bed as if he had never left, a parrot perched on the bedhead. 'Where have you been? You look different—your hair—it's all long and tangled. You're brown. Thin. You've been sleeping rough, haven't you? And what's this?' She'd found the marks of the lash on his back. 'How did you get these? Oh, David!'

The avalanche of words ended in a hug so tight that David could barely breathe. It was easier than he had expected. His mother's relief meant she supplied his own story for him. All he need do was agree.

'You went to look for your father, didn't you? I told the police once if I told them a thousand times, that they should look for you on the south coast. I knew you'd go there. But he's not there, David. I don't know where he is—I'd tell you if I did. It's like he's vanished from the face of the Earth. And when you vanished too—I didn't know what to do. But you're back—that's what matters.'

After inadequately explaining himself to a cross-looking policewoman and sitting through a severe scolding from his grandfather, there didn't seem to be more anyone could say. David had fastened the golden thread to a tree the night before.

He now brought the loose end into his room and tied it to his bedpost (his mother didn't seem able to see it). He hid the scissors and Shushula's lock of hair in his old Lego box, and waited for life to return to normal. Scoldings and disgruntled officers of the law were nothing compared to frappings, walking the plank, and life-and-death duels in the hot sun. If anything, the worst was his mother's silence: she seemed scared that if she told him off, as she normally would have done, he would run away again. He wished he could put her mind at rest but his few attempts only served to make her more worried. In the end he decided he had to wait for it all to blow over, like a storm.

And blow over it did. He had returned in the middle of the half term holidays. When Monday of the first week back at school came, his mother called up the stairs:

'David! Time to go!'

He tucked a lock of silvery hair into his pocket, gave Milli a nut, and ran downstairs.

'Bye, Mum. See you later!'

'I'll be here when you get home. Don't be late.' Her voice shook slightly.

'I won't, I promise.'

His notoriety as the boy who ran away earned David a few hours' respite from Ricko's gang.

232

The children of Mr Barnet's class watched him curiously, half afraid, wondering if he had changed at all in the month he had been missing.

'Where've you been, David?' asked Mike, the quiet boy who often sat next to him.

'I ran away to sea,' he replied, feeling all eyes, including Ricko's, on him.

'No, I mean really.'

'Really.'

Mike looked at him hard then shrugged. 'OK, keep your secret then. Fancy kicking a ball about with us at break?'

David walked down Park Road but he wasn't really seeing it. His mind was with the *Golden Needle*. Where was she now? Had the crew caught up with his father? And the *Scythe*: had they repaired the engines yet? Would they keep to the agreement? He didn't like the fact that, as guardian of the thread, he held Earth's future in his hands, but he was determined to obey orders if he received the signal to cut.

Wham! A bag slammed into David's back, knocking him to his knees.

'I've missed you, wimp,' jeered Ricko. 'So glad you decided to come back for more.'

For a fleeting moment, David experienced his

old feelings of powerlessness and fear when confronted by the gang; but then he remembered the other bullies he had defeated in far worse circumstances than this.

Thwack! He threw his sports bag at Ricko's legs, felling him like a tree. David scrambled to his feet and glared round at the rest of the gang.

'Anyone else want to follow your maggot-brained loser of a leader?' He bunched his fists, arms toned with muscles gained from weeks of deck scrubbing and climbing the rigging. The gang looked confused; one or two were beginning to shuffle away.

'Get him! There's only one of him, you stupid morons!' yelled Ricko as he got back on his feet.

David swallowed. He was going to fight them all if he had to, but he had to admit the odds were not in his favour.

A football sailed over David's head and hit Ricko in the face.

'Oh yeah? Well, not any more, pal,' said Mike, pushing his way through. 'You drove my friend away once. You're not going to this time.'

Ricko wiped his bleeding nose viciously. Still, they're only two, David could see him thinking.

'Out-numbered, Davy?' came a gruff voice as his grandfather used his walking stick to beat a way through to the front of the group. He had come to check his grandson got home in good time.

The presence of an adult took the wind out of Ricko's sails. He seemed to diminish in size, slouching as his eyes darted this way and that to find a way out.

'Out-numbered? I suppose they are, Grandad, as we're worth ten of them,' said David with a grin. 'Rickets, you'd better get lost. But before you go, just remember this: you're not worth a monkey's fart, you with your face like a cow's bum.' It was strange how easily the sailors' salty language tripped off his tongue. 'If you mess with me again, I'll rearrange it into something more pleasing—well, anything would be more pleasing, wouldn't it, Mike?'

'Yeah, I'd say so,' said Mike, stooping to pick up his football. David's grandfather chuckled.

Ricko opened his mouth as if to say something, thought twice, closed it and gave the nod to his gang. The boys ran off in different directions, leaving the passage down Park Road clear for David to sail home.

* * *

Six weeks later, as David and his mother sat down for supper, there was a knock at the front door. She had just finished admiring the necklace of blue shells he had made for her.

'I'll go,' said David. 'It's probably Mike.'

He opened the door. There on the step stood a stranger, smelling of salt and fish, long hair matted on his shoulders, a wild light in his eyes.

'David?' he said tentatively.

'D-Dad? Is that really you?'

'Can I come in?'

David looked over his shoulder. He could see his mother pouring herself a glass of red wine.

'I dunno. I'll have to ask Mum.'

'Who is it, David?' she called. His helpless silence brought her into the hall. 'I said, who is it?'

'It's me, Jean.'

David ducked just in time as a glassful of red wine was thrown in the face of the visitor; he then hastily made room as his mother next threw herself at her husband, sobbing and cursing him.

Ten minutes later the three members of the Jones family sat in awkward silence around the now cold supper.

'So you ran away to sea,' said David's mum quietly. 'Whatever for?'

'There was something I had to do.' Simon glanced over at David. Their eyes met in understanding.

'More important than me—and David?'

He nodded.

'I'm not sure I can forgive you, Simon. I don't understand what could be more important than your family. You don't know what I've been through—what with David disappearing as well—it's been a nightmare.'

'I know, Jean. I'm sorry. I'm sure David is too. I don't expect you to welcome me back. But I've done what I had to do and I'm ready to come home if you'll have me.'

'I'll have to think about it,' she replied, shaking her head.

'Dad, just how did you get back?' David asked quietly as his mother got up to take the dishes into the kitchen. 'Did you meet Captain Fisher?'

He shook his head. 'No, I never got to see him. But I had a very interesting voyage aboard another ship. I met a couple of your friends— they told me what you'd done. I'm proud of you.' He ruffled Davy's hair.

'What, Stella Tor gave you a lift!' marvelled David.

'For you, if you believe it, Davy. "Just this once, for the child's sake," she said and gave me this. She said it should replace what the *Golden Needle* had stolen from you.' David's father put the emerald dagger on the table. 'Only, don't let on to your mother,' he said with a wink. 'I don't think she'd approve.'

'No,' said David, risking a look over his shoulder at his mother standing staring at the unwashed dishes in the sink, 'I don't think she would.'

'Captain Tor said you were to keep it safely hidden until you went to sea again.'

That night, David put the emerald-studded dagger beside the diamond scissors. He touched the thread fastened to his bedpost, feeling it thrum softly beneath his fingertips as if plucked by the waves of the Seas In-between. Go to sea again? Now his father was back to help guard the thread, he might just do that one day.

JULIA GOLDING grew up on the edge of Epping Forest. After reading English at Cambridge, she joined the Foreign Office and served in Poland. Her work as a diplomat took her from the high point of town twinning in the Tatra Mountains to the low of inspecting the bottom of a Silesian coal mine.

On leaving Poland, she joined Oxfam as a lobbyist on conflict issues, campaigning at the United Nations and with governments to lessen the impact of war on civilians living in war zones. She now works as a freelance writer.

Married with three children, she lives in Oxford.